CRY WOLF

A BROWN AND DE LUCA NOVEL

MAGGIE SHAYNE

NEW YORK TIMES BESTSELLING AUTHOR

 Created with Vellum

"This is page-turning, non-stop suspense at its finest. Shayne brings the characters to life for her readers, who will not be disappointed with this fabulously entertaining story." ~**RT Book Reviews** on Innocent Prey

"One of the strongest, most original voices in romance fiction today." ~*New York Times* bestselling author **Anne Stuart**

"Maggie Shayne is a wonderful storyteller. Creepy, chilling, and compelling, her entries into the world of the occult are simply spellbinding!" ~**Heather Graham,** *New York Times* bestselling author

"A moving mix of high suspense and romance, this haunting Halloween thriller will propel readers to bolt their doors at night." ~**Publishers Weekly** on Gingerbread Man.

CHAPTER 1

"This is the first year I've been allowed to come to the fair without grownups," Joshua said. He was walking along the midway, awash in carnival music and the smells of fried foods and horses.

"Are you kidding?" Toby asked. "Man, your family is nuts. I've been coming alone forever. This is like my third year." He ate the last of his cotton candy and tossed the cardboard cone into a nearby wastebasket.

"It's your *second* year," Hunter said. "And you don't come alone, you come with us." Then he shoved the teddy bear he'd just won throwing darts at balloons, into Josh's chest. "Can you fit that in your backpack?"

Toby and Chuckie elbowed each other, grinning.

"It's for my little cousin," Hunter explained as Josh took off his backpack and shoved the purple bear inside. He'd been feeling stupid for bringing one when none of the other guys had. But he'd been carrying their crap around all day, so he guessed it had come in handy. He added the bear to his collection of souvenir slurpy containers, loose change, and Chuck's inhaler.

Josh's best friends were also the three coolest guys in the sixth grade. Seventh grade, once summer vacation was over. Hunter Marks was taller than the others by a solid six inches, and he hadn't been held back even once. He was tougher than any of them. Nobody messed with Hunter, and his basketball skills had earned him the adoration of the entire middle school. Good genes, Josh thought. Toby Gaye took a lot of ribbing for his last name, but he was funny as heck, and that seemed to outweigh it. He was popular by virtue of being the class clown. Chuckie Barnes was the smallest one. He looked like that skinny baby rooster on the cartoons, Foghorn Leghorn's son, right down to the wire-rimmed glasses. His frequent bouts of asthma and scrawny physique would've made him bully bait if he hadn't been part of Hunter and Toby's inner circle.

And now, they'd sort of pulled Josh into their gang. He guessed that made him one of the cool guys now, too. He walked a little taller. After some crazy lady had tried to shoot people at his big brother's graduation party, Josh's popularity among his peers had shot through the roof. And he was glad. His mother being in a nuthouse had been his previous claim to fame. A sniper at a grad party was much cooler. His status, when he entered the seventh grade in a few weeks, was going to be way better than before. And it was about time.

Hitching his backpack up on his shoulders, he nodded toward the scariest ride on the entire midway, the Raptor, and said, "You guys want to go again?"

Each of the guys dug into their pockets to pull out what remained of their ride tickets. Toby had seven, just enough to get on The Raptor one more time. But Hunter was down to two, and Chuck didn't have any.

Josh headed over to the ticket stand, dragged a crumpled twenty-dollar bill out of his pocket, and shoved it through the opening in the plexiglass. A small lady with a chubby hand slid a flat sheet of tickets back out to him, and he started tearing them into strips along the perforations as he rejoined the group, then handed them around.

"Dude, how much money you got on you, anyway?" Hunter asked.

Josh shrugged and Toby said, "Plenty. His parents are like loaded or something. His mom's famous."

"She's not my—I mean, yeah, she *is* kind of famous." They were talking about Rachel, of course, who was not his mother. And Uncle Mason who wasn't his father. But they all lived together, like a real family, so it was close enough. He felt a little guilty about not correcting his friends. But on the other hand, if his friends were starting to forget who his real mother was, then that was a good thing for him, wasn't it?

And his real mom would never know. Right?

The guys took the tickets he gave them. There were three left over, and probably not a ride in the entire park that only took three. Josh looked around, saw a mom with a little kid about four, so he stepped into her path and held them out to her. "You can have these if you want. We're on our last ride for the day anyhow."

She took them and was still looking at him with raised eyebrows when he and the guys walked away to get in line for another round on the Raptor.

"After this, I gotta go," Josh said with a look at his phone. "My brother's picking me up at eight."

"Dude, you could *walk* home from here!" Hunter sounded as if that was a far better option. "Why's he gotta pick you up?"

He was right, of course, but the walk home was two miles over a dirt road that skirted the reservoir on one side and the woods on the other. Seasonal use only. Nobody else on it even in the summer. He hadn't even argued when Uncle Mason had told him that he had to ride home with Jeremy. The idea of walking home that way, after everything that had happened, scared the crap out of him.

Chuck elbowed Hunter. "You've seen his brother's car, though. Who *wouldn't* rather ride in that than walk home?"

The other guys nodded, saving Josh once again from having to explain something that would've been embarrassing. He was still a little bit afraid of the dark, and of long walks on deserted stretches of road in the middle of nowhere. But he didn't want to have to explain all that.

Chuckie grinned at him though, and Josh got the feeling he knew the truth. He smiled back, grateful.

The line moved fast, and the four boys got a car to themselves on one of the four-car pendulums that revolved as they swung higher and higher and higher, maxing out so high they were momentarily suspended upside down and weightless, held in their seats only by the safety bar and each boy's own death grip on it.

It was over way too fast. Josh was proud that he hadn't yelled even once. None of the guys had. But he was a little unsteady on his feet as they got off the ride and headed back onto the midway.

Then he heard a familiar bark—well, you know, the snuffly sound bulldogs call a bark—and looked up to see Myrtle and Hugo galloping toward him. The older blind bulldog, Myrtle, kept her side pressed to the puppy's side the entire way. Hugo was like her seeing-eye pup.

"Aw, dude, cool dogs," Hunter said when Myrtle bashed her iron skull into Josh's shin.

Josh crouched down, petting them both. "Hey, Myrtle, meet the guys. Guys, this is Myrtle. She's blind but she gets around great. And the pup is Hugo."

The guys bent to pet the dogs, too, and Jeremy, who was right behind the dogs, said, "Hey guys. Good day?"

They all straightened, maybe standing a little taller in the presence of Josh's big brother, Jeremy, who was far cooler than any of them by virtue of his advanced age, recent graduation, and classic ride.

"The best," Toby said.

"It was all right," Hunter said at the same time.

Chuckie stayed crouched, petting the dogs, talking to them like they were people.

"Any of you guys need a ride home?" Jeremy asked.

"We brought our bikes," Hunter said.

"Okay, that's cool. You ready, Josh?"

"Yep. See you guys. C'mon, Myrt."

Myrt abandoned Hugo to press herself against Josh's leg and they wound their way back to the parking lot and climbed into Jeremy's Iroc Z. Jere revved the motor a little, showing off for the guys while he waited for traffic to clear so he could pull out and to the left. A quarter mile later, he took a right at the stoplight, and kept going until the pavement ended, and the woods began on the left, the reservoir's sloping shore on the right.

Two miles up on the left was where they lived in a giant camper with Aunt Rachel and Uncle Mason. His friends were right about Rachel. She was loaded, and so after the firebug had torched her house, she'd picked out the biggest, fanciest camper he'd ever seen. It had four slide-out sections, a satellite dish, three TVs, and a patio. It sat on the front lawn about fifty yards from the house, which was in the process of being rebuilt.

It was pretty cool how they'd all sat down together, throwing out ideas while Uncle Mason sketched pictures and Aunt Rachel took notes. She said this time, the house was gonna be *their* dream home, not just hers, because they were all living there together from now on.

He guessed that meant she and Uncle Mace were official. And he was glad.

Josh's room was gonna be a gamer's paradise. Jeremy was getting an apartment over the garage, so he would have his own space during breaks from college, which started in just a couple of weeks. Right now their dream house was just a big empty shell, but they'd only been working on it just over a month.

It was August 1st, and life was changing. Life had been changing for him and Jeremy for a couple of years now, but this time, he thought it was changing into something really awesome. And it was about time, too.

Jere parked the car near the camper and cut the motor. Josh opened his door, and the puppy dove out of the car and stood on the ground barking like mad. Josh helped Myrtle out, picking her right up and then setting her on the ground. "Jere, I think she's getting lighter." Then he frowned. "And look, her neck rolls aren't covering up her collar anymore."

"Shh. Don't let Rachel hear you say that or—"

"Don't let Rachel hear you say what?" Rachel said, coming out the camper's little door and dropping into a crouch as Myrtle raced toward her. She caught the dog's face in her hands before she got her shins bashed. Good trick, Josh thought.

"That Myrtle's losing some of her chub," he told her. "I guess the Dr. Clive was right." Josh noticed Jeremy wincing and closing his eyes.

Rachel frowned. "Dr. Clive was *not* right," she said. "Myrtle isn't losing weight. She's in perfect shape, and has been all along. Cutting out the tiny little tastes we feed her from our dinner plates—"

"And lunch plates," Jeremy said, "and breakfast plates, and bedtime snacks, and cheese sticks. Don't forget the cheese sticks."

"—hasn't made one bit of difference," Rachel continued, after sending Jeremy a lovingly withering glare. "Because we haven't been giving her enough to *make* a difference. She wasn't overweight. That vet is full of shi...blue mud."

"Right. I hear a lot of Cornell-educated vets are," Jeremy added a smile, then before Rachel could respond, said, "Yo, Josh, get your crap outta my car, huh?"

Josh turned back toward the car, but Rachel was still talking. "Myrtle is just the right size for a big-boned bulldog," she said, rubbing Myrt's ears just the way she liked best. "Aren't you, Myrt? Yes, you are."

The bulldog wiggled her butt, because she didn't have a tail. Just a curly little stub on her backside. Although, Josh thought that curly stub was protruding from her rump more than before. Yeah, she had definitely lost weight.

He reached into Jeremy's car, picked his backpack up

from the seat, and then said, "Aw, crap!" Rachel and Jeremy both turned his way, waiting for the rest.

"I forgot, I've got all the guys' stuff in my backpack."

"Anything that can't wait until tomorrow?" Rachel asked. Josh pulled out Chuckie's inhaler, held it up, and she said, "Nope, guess not."

"I'll take him, Aunt Rache," Jeremy offered. "If we hurry, we can catch them before they even get home."

"Thanks Jeremy." Rachel clasped her hands near her chin and batted her eyes. "You're so selfless."

"Yeah, and you love driving your car anywhere for any reason," Josh added.

"You reap most of the benefits of that, squirt. Hop in."

"Make it quick," Rachel said. "And by quick, I mean keeping to the speed limit, Jere. You know, within reason."

He sent her a nod and got behind the wheel. Josh buckled up, and the car headed right back the way it had come from, rumbling and growling to the end of their road and then left through the village.

"So who lives closest?" Jere asked.

"Hunter. The next road on the right." The other guys lived farther along the main drag, Chuckie on the left, and Toby a little farther, on a dirt side road not unlike Josh's own.

Jeremy turned onto Hunter's road. "How far up?"

"Not far. Top of the hill and then around a sharp curve, and then–wait, wait. Jeremy stop!"

Jere hit the brakes right in the middle of the road and

sent Josh his patented WTF look, but Josh was already trying to open the door, and then he finally did and got out and ran to the bike he'd spotted lying on its side in the ditch. He scrambled down to it, his feet splashing into the water that ran in the bottom. "It's Hunter's bike!"

"Holy crap." Jeremy was out of the car, too, looking left and right, and shouting, "Hunter! Hunter, where the heck are you?"

Josh started to reach for the bike to pull it out of the mud, but he stopped when he saw what looked like blood on the handlebar. "Jere?"

His big bro was right behind him by then. "Don't touch it, Josh. He probably tried some BMX move or something and crashed. Probably limped home for a Band-Aid." He was pulling out his phone, and a second later, said, "What's his number?"

"I have it on my phone." Josh was trembling as he pulled his phone out of his pocket, scrolled to Hunter's entry and tapped the button to call his landline. The water was starting to seep into his sneakers. Mrs. Marks picked up on the second ring.

"Just ask if he's there," Jere whispered. "Don't scare her. We don't know if there's a reason to yet."

Nodding in a jerky motion, Josh said, "Hey, Miz Marks, it's Josh. Is Hunter home?"

"No, but I expect him soon. I told him before dark, so he should be here any minute. Weren't you at the fair with him?"

"Uh, yeah, but I went home and realized he left some stuff in my backpack."

"Oh, well, did you try texting him?"

"I didn't uh...didn't think of that. Thanks, Miz Marks." He ended the call, and looked up at Jeremy, who was already making a call of his own, and Josh hoped it was to Uncle Mason. Jere put his phone on speaker, and held it between the two of them.

While it rang, Jere said, "Hunter's probably still walking. Maybe he crashed his bike within the last few minutes, and he just hasn't made it home yet."

"It's not that far," Josh said, looking up the hill. He could see the beginning of the curve. Hunter's house was just the other side of it.

"Hey, Jere, what's up?" Uncle Mason's voice came from the phone speaker. Just hearing it made Josh feel a little better.

Jere nodded at him, a sort of it's-gonna-be-okay kind of nod, and said, "Hey, Uncle Mace. Um, Josh's friend Hunter was riding his bike home from the fair, last we knew. But we just found his bike in a ditch down the road from his house, and his mom says he's not home yet."

"Where's Josh? Are you safe?"

"I'm right here, Uncle Mace. We're fine."

"We're by the bike now," Jeremy said. "Right where we found it."

"Okay, stay there for now, but get in the car and lock it.

Don't touch the bike. Does Hunter have a cell?" Uncle Mason asked.

"Just an iPod, but he can text with it," Josh said. "Uncle Mason, there's blood on the handlebar." He hated how hard his voice was shaking.

"I'm on my way, Josh. I'm gonna be right there. Five minutes. Get in the car and lock it, just to be on the safe side. Anyone besides me shows up, you just drive away, okay?"

"We'll drive up and down the road," Jeremy said. "See if we spot him walking or..." He shot a quick look at Josh. "...or anything."

"Okay. Do that. I'll be there soon."

Jeremy pocketed his phone and said, "Come on, let's get back in the car, kiddo."

But Josh had turned to look back at the bike in the ditch and kind of got stuck there. He couldn't even blink. "It's like we're contagious," he said.

"What do you mean?" Standing right behind him, Jeremy dropped his hand on Josh's shoulder. He had big hands all of the sudden, Josh realized. His hands were grown-up hands. When had that happened?

"It's like we've got some kind of curse on us or something, and now it's spreading to our friends. I've only been hanging out with Hunter for a month, and it's already got him."

"Aw come on, Josh." Jere tugged on his shoulder until he turned Josh around. "You know there's no curse. We've had some bad luck, that's all. This is probably nothing. Hunter's probably fine, prob'ly knocked a tooth out on his handlebar and ran home crying."

"Not Hunter. Hunter doesn't cry." Josh looked up at his brother and said, "Something bad happened to him, Jere. I feel it, right here." He pressed a fist into his belly and tried to keep breathing past the knot in his throat. "And I don't know how, but I think it's because of us."

"Shoot, you're starting to act like you're the one with NFP."

His reference to Aunt Rachel's gift, which she called NFP for not effing psychic, made Josh smile, and his heart felt a little bit lighter.

CHAPTER 2

RACHEL

I rode to the spot with Mason, and my heart about broke when we pulled up close enough to see the look on Josh's face. He was trying hard not to cry, the poor kid. He'd had a growth spurt over the summer, was two inches taller than me now, and wearing shoes as big as Mason's. But inside he was still a kid, all of twelve years old, with a hundred or so years' worth of trauma already loaded up. And now here came some more.

"He'll be okay," Mason said, reading me as well as I could usually read everyone else. "He's a tough kid."

"He shouldn't have to be." I got out of the car. The police hadn't arrived yet. Well, technically Mason was the police, but he was off duty. He'd called it in. The Broome

County Sheriff's department and the New York State Troopers were both on the way. But we were there first.

Of all the times for my NFP to fail me! I was furious with myself.

Probably not the best state of mind to get your stuff working, there Rache.

I know, Inner Bitch. I know.

I went right up to Josh and hugged him, thinking it was probably the last thing he wanted me to do. But he proved me wrong, hugged me hard.

Mason and Jeremy were over by the bike, not touching, but talking low. Jeremy was going to be a cop like his uncle. And he'd be a good one, too. They were looking at tire marks on the shoulder of the road.

"I gotta let the guys know," Josh said. "I can't believe this. We were all together an hour ago."

"We'd better let his mom know first," I said, because she was heading down the road toward us. I'd met Hunter's mom and dad at his birthday party. She was a stay-at-home mom who was always selling something online. His dad was a math teacher over at Whitney Point Central.

"Man, what are we gonna tell her?" Josh looked at me with round eyes. "What do you think happened to him, Aunt Rache?"

"I don't know, hon."

"Well, yeah, but can't you...you know." He wiggled his fingers at his head, like that meant anything.

"It's been a little blocked up lately."

He lifted his eyebrows high. "Your stuff is gone?"

"Not gone, just...down." Mrs. Marks–I couldn't remember her first name–had picked up the pace, and I didn't need my NFP to see the worry on her face. "What's happened? What are you all doing here?" She spotted the bike and heard the siren at the same instant, and then she just froze where she was, and her hand fluttered up toward her mouth. "Where is my son?" It came out all strained and soft.

Mason came up out of the ditch, thank God. I was no good at soothing people. He was way better.

"We don't know exactly what's happened here, Mrs. Marks. But I don't think there's any need to panic. Josh and Jeremy were on their way to return some things Hunter left in Josh's backpack, and they spotted his bike in the ditch."

"But where is he?" She looked at the bike, looked at Josh, then looked up and down the road. A police car pulled up. Jeremy was standing near the tire marks they'd been looking at, and he signaled the driver to stop before he made it there.

"Did you call the police?" she asked Mason. "Why did you call the police? Where is Hunter?"

"We don't know, Chelsea," he said, putting hands on her shoulders.

Chelsea. That was her first name. How does he remember every little thing like he does?

"He might've knocked his head, and wandered off, a little loopy. We'll find him. Why don't you let me talk to the officers, and uh...maybe you should call Glenn, okay?"

She pressed her hands to her head, like she was trying to keep it from exploding.

"I remember when Jeremy and Josh went missing last year," I said, trying for empathy. "I know how scary this is."

She looked at me, eyes so vacant I didn't think she'd even heard me. I tried again. "Do you have your phone with you, or...?"

She shook her head, looking past me, so I looked too. Mason and the other cops were looking at the bike, at the ground around the bike. One of them pulled out a Q-tip and dabbed at the blood on the handlebar.

Not good. I moved a little to block her view, and said, "That's okay. I have mine. I'll call him for you. Can you tell me his number?"

"What are they doing?" she asked.

I waved a hand. "Oh, you know, cop stuff. They're always overly—"

She pushed past me, running right down into the ditch, just as one of the cops said, "There's something in there."

Something in where? I went to Chelsea Marks, who had frozen with her feet in the muck, as Mason used a pencil to fish a rolled-up piece of paper out of the hollow handlebar, which was missing its grip. He held up the pencil with the paper around it.

"What...what is that?" Hunter's mom asked.

One of the officers handed Mason a latex glove. He didn't even put it on, just used it to grip the corner, and unroll the paper, far enough to read what was written there.

"'Wait for instructions.'"

"That's it?" Jeremy asked.

"What? What is it, what does that mean?" Chelsea Marks was on the edge of losing it, I thought. "Who put that there, what's going on?"

The officer who'd brought Mason the glove, held open an evidence bag, and Mason dropped the note inside, handed her the glove, and then came over to the trembling woman, and said. "We're gonna go up to your house now, Chelsea. We're gonna need to look at Hunter's room, and his computer."

"What does that mean?" she demanded. "Wait for instructions. What does that mean? Tell me!"

"I'm afraid someone might've taken him, Chelsea."

She blinked, like he wasn't speaking a language she knew, and then she whispered, "You mean...he's been kidnapped?"

"It's...possible."

She burst into hysterical tears. They exploded from her, like the dam that had been holding them had broken.

For the next few days, the whole town, hell, the whole county, was out in droves. Citizen volunteers searched the farm fields and state forests while State Police divers explored the Otselic and Tioghnioga Rivers and the reservoir. Mason said that note was a good sign. If whoever had Hunter wanted ransom, then they probably weren't pedophiles. It was truly the best-case scenario. Choosing the son of a stay-at-home mom and a teacher dad as their road to riches wasn't the brightest move, but criminals didn't become criminals because of their stunning intellect.

Or the note was a ruse, so we'd be looking the other way while they did what they wanted to the poor fucking kid and—

No. No, I couldn't even go there.

The boys and I had spent two days searching the area for Hunter along with everyone else. But I knew we weren't going to find him. I mean, not for sure. My knowing-for-sure-thing had been off line for a couple of weeks now, and it was bugging me more than I liked to admit.

It bothered me even more when I saw the headline in the morning paper. *Celebrity Psychic Natalia DaVine To Assist Search for Missing Boy*

I picked up a copy to take with me to see Mason at work, so I'd be able to shake it and slap it onto his desk for emphasis.

"What the fuck, Mason?" I asked, slapping it onto his desk for emphasis.

"Hey, hey, swear jar, remember?"

"There's no swear jar at the Binghamton PD. And so I repeat, what the fuck?"

"Rachel, this is not my fault," Mason said, bringing my focus back to the matter at hand. "I'm not the one who brought her in."

"Fine, then I'll have it out with the chief." It wasn't even a BPD case, really. But this had become a multi-department case. I headed through the beehive to the office of the gorgeous chief whose life I'd sort of saved a year ago. Every cop in the place was looking at me, because I'd made a scene.

When do you not?

Shut up, Inner Bitch. This is not the time.

Mason's hand closed on my shoulder. He had great hands, my guy. Big, strong, manly hands. I usually liked them on me. Anywhere on me. But not today.

"Babe, just listen, will you?"

"You cannot *babe* your way out of this, Mason. I am incensed, insulted and infuriated."

"I can see that." He took my upper arm to try to steer me into a more private room, but I yanked free. Two more steps took me to Chief Vanessa Cantone's office door, where I knocked twice, then walked in.

Rude much?

Yes, IB, I kind of am.

Yeah, you kind of are.

The chief looked up at me, perfect brows raised—and they were perfect. I could never get mine to look like that. And then the surprise faded and the chief leaned back in her chair, sighing. "Hey, Rachel. Been expecting you. You want to sit down?"

"No. I do not want to sit down. What I do want is to know why *my* police department has hired some phony-ass, press-seeking, celebrity psychic to find Hunter Marks."

Chief Cantone met Mason's eyes, nodded at the door. He closed it.

"This is *my* job, Vanessa. And you know it."

"I do know it," she said. "And so does Mason. And no one else."

She had put a pinprick in my balloon there, but I wasn't deflated yet. I was too wound up to go down that easy. "Not true. Mason's kids know. My sister and her perfect husband and the twins know. Myrtle knows."

"Relatives and bulldogs don't count."

"Amy knows."

"Goth-chick personal assistants don't count, either. Look, Rachel, you told me that being a fluff bunny self-help author–" I sent her a look more toxic than a Chernobyl breeze. "Your words, not mine," the chief added quickly. "You told me that the world has enough trouble taking you seriously because of your Positive Polly Persona–long live the gods of irony. You said coming out as some kind of psychic crime solver would ruin your lucrative self-help career."

"I am Not. Fucking. Psychic."

"I know." She sighed. "Look, Natalia DaVine has helped police–"

"Natalia DaVine. Psssh. If she's for real I'll go on the same diet as my bulldog."

"Natalia DaVine has helped police solve seven kidnappings all over the country. She walks in here after we have a kid gone missing. She offers to help. In front of the distraught parents, she does this. What was I supposed to do?"

She got out of her chair, paced to the window, looked outside. "Sorry Miz DaVine, but we have our own Not Fucking Psychic who'd be mad as hell if we accepted your help. Who? Sorry, can't say. She's a very private Not Fucking Psychic, you see."

Most of the air had escaped my balloon by then. I sank into the chair in front of the desk.

"She's right, Rache," Mason said.

"I know she's right. I hate it, but I know." I heaved a sigh. "I don't like this woman, Vanessa. I don't think she's for real–"

"Have you even met her?"

"What's that got to do with anything? Look, you can't let her come in here and give you bullshit leads. You'll be chasing shadows while some pervert has his way with that poor kid."

Vanessa's eyes jerked away from mine on that last line. They focused on the photo on her desk, of her wife and their little girl, and then she looked at a spot on the wall instead. "I'm a good cop, Rachel. So's Mason, and so is Rosie."

"Uh, Chief?" Mason said. "Rosie and I are homicide detectives. And this isn't our case."

"Yeah, well, we're creating an inter-departmental task force to find Hunter Marks, and you're heading it up." She smiled at me. "That way, your girlfriend here can help by being Not Fucking Psychic *privately*."

She let a couple of seconds tick by, probably waiting for me to apologize. You know, unless she'd ever met me.

Finally, she said, "Are we good here? Cause I have a day job, you know."

I lifted my head. "We're good."

"Good. Have a nice day."

Mason opened the door and held it. I got up, straightened my blouse and walked out with as much dignity as I could muster. I'd been wrong. I'd lost my temper. Wasn't the first time, wouldn't be the last. I was feeling pretty remorseful, to be honest. Right up until *she* walked in.

I recognized her, as would anyone who'd ever spent any time in a supermarket checkout line. Natalia's face often graced the covers of the rags in the periodicals rack. She looked like she ought to be baking cookies for a dozen grandchildren. Her hair was dyed a color so bright it was best described as maroon, worn in a poufy style that expanded her head circumference by several inches, curving inward about mid-neck. You know, like a hair helmet. She was round, and wore a multicolored kaftan beneath a floor-length crocheted sweater, and black lace-up boots.

Okay, the boots were kind of cool.

She was as well-known as I was in the non-fiction publishing game, maybe a little bit more. But she was a phony.

And yeah, I used to think of myself as a phony, too, with my positive-thinking, everything-happens-for-a-reason spiel. But as it turned out, my methods worked.

Natalia DaVine was just a fake. I knew she was a fake, because I did not believe in psychics. It was bullshit. All of it.

Natalia walked right past us before I had the chance to close my eyes and try to get a feel for her...a vibe or whatever. Being blind for twenty years, I'd learned how to read people without seeing them, and now that I could see them, the visual tended to drown out everything else. I had to shut it down to really know who anybody was. You know, when it was working.

But I hadn't acted fast enough, and Natalia was already clicking her boots toward Vanessa's office.

"I should stay," I said. "Maybe talk to her, see if I can—"

"Yeah, no." Mason slung an arm around my shoulders and walked me right out through the large door and into the hallway with its gleaming tiles and police chief portraits and funky light fixtures from the 1800s.

I looked up at him, ready to be angry.

"Doesn't Myrtle have a vet's appointment this morning?" He smiled at me, flashing the dimple of doom, damn him. It melted me every time.

"Yeah, she does. Stupid vet and his stupid dietary suggestions."

"She's lost weight, Rachel. You can't deny it."

"No way. All this denying her bites of my dinner and between meal treats is bull. I barely gave her any to begin with. It wasn't enough to make a difference."

"And yet you've been diligently following Dr. Clive's guidelines."

"Just to prove his incompetent ass wrong. Myrtle is big boned. Period. And once I've proven my point, I'm going to find her a new vet. One who agrees with me that life is short and should be savored, and that putting a bulldog on a diet is equivalent to animal abuse."

I glanced down at my watch. Butterfly wings opened to tell me I had to go. And yet I hesitated. "Is there anything new on Hunter?"

"Forensics found nothing on the note or the bike. Blood on the handlebar was Hunter's, but not enough to suggest a serious injury. We've checked up on every sex offender on the registry. So far, they're all accounted for." He sighed heavily, searching my face, about to ask if I had come up with anything.

I shook my head before he did. "It's like my signal's gone down or something."

"We're all crammed together in that camper. You don't have any space."

"I don't think that's it. I think maybe...maybe it's gone, Mace. What if it's gone?"

No sooner had I said it than I heard a shout from back in the squad room. We'd stopped halfway down the hall, and we both raced back there. Mason had his gun in his hand before we burst through the door.

Natalia DaVine stood in the center of the room, holding her hands to either side of her head, shouting "No!" over and over.

Rosie, Mason's partner, was the first to reach her. Actually, he was the only one who tried. Most of the other cops were shaking their heads or rolling their eyes. Chief Cantone stood in the open doorway of her office, looking like she had the mother of all headaches. Rosie gripped the fraud's plump shoulders with his own plump hands and said, "Miss DaVine! You okay, Miss DaVine?"

She opened her eyes, but all that showed were the whites, because she'd rolled them so far back in her head. Rosie jumped away from her, cussing like...well, like me. Then DaVine brought her eyeballs back around, and staring sightlessly said, "Trees. He's near trees. Tall. Pines. Yes, pines!"

"Um, yeah, have you looked outside?" I asked. "We're *all* near tall pines. This whole county is near tall pines."

She blinked as if she'd just awoken from a dream, and turned her kind brown eyes my way. And then she smiled, "Rachel de Luca?"

Shit, she recognized me. We'd never met, but we had been in the same room once or twice, back in the day when we'd both been budding upstarts in the book biz, attending every conference and convention there was. Thank God I didn't have to do that anymore. Networking. Gag me.

I swallowed and said, "Hello, Natalia. Nice to finally meet you." *Not.*

She came closer, clasped my hand in both of her too-warm ones, and held on too long.

"Oh, this is perfect. Perfect! With your positive attitude and my gift, we're far more likely to have a good outcome." She turned toward the chief, still gripping my hand. "The boy is still alive. And I believe he's unharmed. He's being held somewhere very wooded."

"I'm afraid that doesn't narrow it down much, Miss DaVine," Vanessa said.

"I know, I know. But I think if one of your officers could drive me around for a while, I might—"

"I really don't have that kind of manpower," Vanessa said. Then she looked right at me, and she got the most evil smile on her face that I had ever seen in my life. "Maybe Rachel would like to volunteer for the job."

"I...have...something... Myrtle! That's right, Myrtle's

appointment. How could I forget? I have a vet's appointment and I really can't miss it. Myrtle is my–"

"Dog," Natalia said, like it proved her skills. Shit, she had a nearly fifty-fifty shot, there right?

Say iguana. Do it, say iguana, my Inner Bitch advised.

But Natalia went on before I got the word out. "When's the appointment?"

Oh, come on. I am not going to do this. I sent Vanessa a look that told her there would be vengeance, and possibly bloodshed, and said, "In an hour."

"I can wait," the phony psychic said. "Pick me up when you're finished?"

I sighed heavily, looked to Mason for help, but he only shrugged. So I said, "Fine. Where are you staying?"

Everything happens for a reason, Inner Bitch chirped inside my head.

If she had been real, I'd have smacked the smile right off her face.

CHAPTER 3

Myrtle wore her leopard print goggles and matching scarf, and sat in the passenger side of my Thunderbird. I put the top down, which she loved, and made her wear her special doggy seatbelt, which she detested. When we drove past McDonald's, she tipped her head back and sniffed the air.

"I know, baby. Stupid vet and his stupid diet. Once I prove him wrong, I'll take you for lunch."

At the word lunch, she faced me fast. She couldn't see, but you'd never know it. Her nostrils twitched as she sniffed for evidence of anything yummy. Or remotely edible.

"Hang in there, girl." I pulled into the parking lot, and she waited for me to come around the car to open her door and help her down. She was a diva, no question. The sun was low, and slanting right into her face, so I left her tinted goggles on, and snapped on her sparkly leash that was more an accessory than a necessity. She walked close to my side, so my leg brushed her with every step. We went right inside.

"Ah, there you are, Ms. de Luca," said the young woman at the desk. She already had Myrtle's file folder in front of her. "This won't take a minute." She came out from behind the chest-high counter and walked us right over to a scale near the wall. It was a metal platform, only a couple of inches off the floor. There was a digital panel on the wall above it, connected by a cord.

I picked Myrtle up, took off her goggles and set her on the platform. She turned around slowly, sniffing the non-skid surface and not liking it. "She'll settle in a second. Myrt, sit down."

"Ahh, Rachel and Myrtle! How are you?" Dr. Clive came from the back with his usual friendly smile on his face. Clive's last name was Hwang, pronounced "wong." No one ever got it right. To avoid the irritation of everyone calling him "Dr. Wang" he just went by Dr. Clive.

Had it been me, I'd have put a poster on the wall that read, "If you're not saying Wong, you're saying it wrong." But no one asked.

"You've been following the diet?" he asked, coming to join us at the scale as the digits dithered.

"No between meal snacks. No people food. No fun. No reason to live. Yes, religiously."

"Really?"

I shrugged. "Mostly."

Myrt laid down all at once, and the digital panel went temporarily insane, then settled down at 62.5

I frowned at it. "What did she weigh last time?"

"Seventy-two," Dr. Clive said, taking the folder from his receptionist. "And we used the same scale."

"Seventy-two?" I blinked in disbelief. "She's down ten pounds?" He nodded, as happy as if he'd just won a prize. He really loved dogs, our vet. I loved everything about him...except this.

It was true, then. I had made my dog fat. Ten pounds is a lot when you're a bulldog. I looked at Myrtle, really looked at her. And then I frowned hard and leaned down. "Oh my God, I think I see a rib! Maybe she's sick!"

"She's not sick, Rachel. She was fat. Now she's a lean, mean bulldog machine." He leaned down, scratching Myrt's ears just the way she loved best. "Who's a lean mean bulldog? You are, that's who." Myrt tipped her head sideways, pressing against his hand. "Her tail is even an outie again!"

"Oh, for crying out loud."

Dr. Clive straightened, and went back behind the counter, jotted the new weight into the file, and slapped it closed. "You're all set. Keep up the good work. You're doing great, Rachel."

"Yeah. I uh...what if she loses too much?"

"She's fine. We'll just keep track. You can add a healthy treat here and there, just don't overdo it. And no people food. If she starts gaining, we'll cut back again. She's at a very healthy weight right where she is."

I was deflated. I had loved my bulldog into obesity. Poor pup. I put her back into her seat and drove her home, and after she'd had a healthy meal and a walk, she curled up in her dog bed and was out like a light.

Josh and Hugo were at Mason's mother's for the day. But Myrtle would be fine in the big camper by herself. She was an independent woman.

I'd taught her well.

And now, I thought, I'm going to take my independent ass to pick up an irritating phony baloney psychic and drive her around aimlessly to keep her out of everyone's hair. Vanessa and Mason had better appreciate this.

***

"So how is your dog? Myrtle, right?" Natalia DaVine asked.

The semi-famous psychic was in the passenger seat of my T-bird. Myrtle's seat. I'd called to check on Josh at his grandmother's house. She said she was worried. All he was doing was playing video games.

"When isn't he playing video games?" I'd asked.

She said he wasn't wearing his headset, jumping out of his seat and yelling to other gamers. He was just staring blankly at the screen, his fingers and thumbs on the paddle moving almost on their own.

Muscle memory. It's like cellular memory. Ask me about it sometime.

I glanced at my passenger and found her looking at me expectantly. Right, she'd asked about Myrtle. "She's down ten pounds," I said. "I think the vet's scales need calibration."

Her eyebrows formed sideways question marks and she tilted her head.

I nodded at the two Diet Cokes between us. "I brought you one, if you're thirsty."

She pressed a hand to her chest and pulled her chin inward, like she was trying to shrink away from the toxic brew. "Thank you, no. I try not pollute my temple."

I sent her a doubtful look and she smiled. "It dulls my receptors," she said, touching her fingers to her temples. "I find my visions are much clearer when I stay away from processed foods and chemicals. I eat natural and organic to the greatest extent possible."

For a second, I wondered if junk food was what was clouding up my own signal. Then I reminded myself she was a fraud, and took a great big gulp from my probably HDPE-or-whatever-the-bad-kind-is plastic bottle. Which I would recycle. I mean a nickel's a fucking nickel, am I right?

"So how do your uh…your powers work?" I asked. No warning, no working up to it. You get honest answers when you don't prepare people for your questions. Just spring it on them. It's like truth serum.

She looked at me quickly. I kept my eyes on the road, and felt her wondering whether I was asking in a sarcastic, doubting-Thomasina sort of way or really wanted to know. So, I sent her a smile to ease her mind.

"It's complicated. When there's something I need to know, I go through a mental process that triggers my brain to relax into alpha state. It's a sort of visualization-slash-meditation I've perfected over the years to open my third eye."

Ah-huh. Okay. If someone had asked me the same question I'd have answered, "Damned if I know. Shit just pops in."

"I'd love to know that process." Did I say that out loud?

"I can write it down and email it to you," she said. "But each person is unique, and has to develop her own methods."

"Oh. Pssh. Yeah, sure, I mean, I wasn't asking because I wanted to try it or anything. I just, uh—" I blew air past my lower lip to make a motor sound. "I'm just curious about all this...woo woo sort of stuff."

"Most people are." She patted my hand on the steering wheel, like she was reassuring me that I hadn't offended her with my curiosity. She had no idea I was looking for holes in her story.

"So, what has your third eye told you about Hunter Marks?"

Again, she sent me that sideways glance. "Woods. North. Close. Safe."

I waited for her to go on. She didn't. I looked at her, then at the road, then at her again. "That's it?"

She nodded. "I'm not getting anything more yet. We are heading north, aren't we?"

"Yep."

She pinched her forehead right in the middle and squished her eyes shut tight. Then she opened them again. "Rachel, do you have a map?"

I thought it was an odd request, but nodded down at my aftermarket in-dash touchscreen. Alpine. Spared no expense.

She was shaking her head before I finished tapping the map icon. "I mean a paper one."

"I think I left it home with my abacus."

Her frown was quick and deep. "You don't like me, do you?"

I lifted my brows. "Actually, you're growing on me."

"Then what's the source of this hostility I sense emanating from you?"

It was not proof of her skills. I manage to let *everyone* feel my hostility without a word. It's a gift.

"I'm worried that your involvement in this case could put Hunter in more danger than he already is."

She held my gaze, not flinching. "And?" she prompted.

Yeah, I'd bitten my lip at the end there, to keep the rest in, but hell, she'd literally asked for it. "If that turns out to be true, then I'm going to expose you as a fraud."

"Wow." She was quiet for a moment, then she said, "Well, thanks for the candor. Pull in there, will you?"

I looked in the direction she'd pointed, flipped on the signal and pulled in at a convenience store. She got out and went inside. I sat there drumming my fingers on the steering wheel and waiting. I tried to feel guilty for being nasty to her, but there wasn't a bit of remorse in me. I hadn't said anything but the truth.

I wonder what that process of hers is that gets her juices flowing.

No, you don't, Inner Bitch.

Yes, I do. And so do you. You wonder if it would work for us. Come on, admit it.

It wouldn't work for us because A. We're Not Fucking Psychic, and B. Neither is she.

But what if she is?

Shut up, Inner Bitch.

It was nice out. I put the top down and wondered if my passenger would mind. I wondered what that helmet hair of hers would look like blown around a little.

After a few minutes, Natalia came out of the store with a bottle of apple juice and a spiral bound Central New York Street Atlas. She got back into the car without a word about the top being down, buckled up and immediately opened the book, and started flipping pages. She kept it up for a few pages, then slapped the cover closed and leaned her head back on the seat.

"You all right over there?" I asked.

She started humming and rocking. I saw one of Josh's teachers come out of the store, glance our way and do a comical double take at the nutcase in my passenger seat. I gave her a dainty finger wave and hit the button to put the top back up. Bitch was embarrassing me.

Once the top was secure, I hit the road again. Natalia's humming had gone softer, and her eyes were open and rolled back in her head.

"That helps, huh? Rolling your eyes like that?" I asked.

She pretended she couldn't hear me, but I felt her react to my words. No humming or rocking required, thanks very much. At least that part of my "gift" hadn't deserted me. I could still read people.

Suddenly, Natalia whipped the book open, brought her head down, opened her eyes wide, and poked a spot on a map with her forefinger. She did it all in one burst of motion that scared me so bad I almost went off the road. Then she blinked as if she'd only just regained consciousness, and looked at where her finger was. "Dog Hollow State Forest," she read. Then she frowned at the book. "It's in Cortland County."

I glanced her way. "What about it?"

"It's where we have to go. Is it far?"

I shrugged and looked at the page. The atlas covered a vast portion of NY State, ranging from the Canadian Border all the way south to the edge of Pennsylvania. It covered several counties. But the page she'd opened to was the county next door. "It's about forty minutes away."

"Will you take me there?"

I mulled on that.

You really think it's smart to go out into some remote patch of wilderness with a lady who might be a little bit off her rocker, there, Skippy?

Um, no, Inner Bitch, I do not. And Skippy? Seriously?

"Maybe I should call Mason," I said. My thumb hit the voice-command button on the steering wheel before I said the final two words.

"We don't need to bother him until we know–"

"Calling Mason Brown," said my car.

I sent Natalia an apologetic smile. "Oops. Darn technology."

"What's up, babe?"

That was Mason's typical greeting when I called him, and I loved it. The sound of his sexy voice calling me babe tickled the irritation right off my spine. My muscles unclenched a little. "I want to report the Dr. Clive for fraud."

"She lost that much, huh?"

"Ten pounds. Mason, I'm afraid she might be seriously ill."

"Right. She caught three froggies yesterday." No one in our family ever said the word "frogs." They were "froggies" because that was the word Myrtle recognized. Froggies were her favorite. "That bulldog feels like a pup again," Mason went on. "You're gonna have to make peace with the fact that the vet was right and we were wrong."

And by *we* he meant *me*. He had agreed with the doc from the beginning. "Never," I said. "Anyway, I'm with Natalia DaVine and you're on speaker. We're heading out to Dog Hollow State Forest."

He took an extra beat to answer and I felt his concern and knew what he was thinking. Not because of my oddball gift, but because we were so tight it was starting to feel like our brains were operating off the same hard drive. So he worried, and I felt mushy inside, and then he said, "Why?"

I flipped my hand, palm up toward Natalia, as in "take it away."

"I feel like we'll find something there," she said, leaning toward the touchscreen as if the speaker was there. It wasn't. "I can't really explain beyond that."

"All right, I'll meet you out there." Mason paused, then said, "Rachel, I'll text you where to meet me, all right?"

That wasn't all he was going to text me. I got that loud and clear. "Okay Mace. See you soon." I hit the disconnect, and before I'd gone another hundred feet down the road my cell phone pinged its text chime, and despite that I was driving, I glanced at the screen.

"I'm 30 min farther than u. Drive around. Kill some time. But do not go to that forest without me."

I typed back, OK, which was about all I could key in without pulling the car over.

I got it. He didn't want me alone in the woods with a woman who thought she was a psychic, because clearly anyone who thought themselves psychic was a few bricks shy of a full load. I'd be insulted by that assumption if I didn't agree with it completely.

I kept driving and watched the clock. Ten minutes out, I said, "Ah, hell, I need to gas this baby up. I don't know why I didn't think of it when we stopped for the map."

Natalia frowned at my dashboard. "It looks like your tank is full."

"Gauge is busted." No, it wasn't. I tapped the glass for good measure. "I never really know how much gas is in the tank. Better safe than sorry, though. We wouldn't want to run out up there in the middle of nowhere. There's nothing on the way, either." Yes, there was.

I pulled a U-turn and headed back the way we'd come. Then I took my sweet time topping off my already nearly-full tank, using the restroom, and re-supplying my Diet Coke.

I figured if I drove slowly back up 26 to Cincy, and then crept slow over back roads to the middle-of-nowhere state forest, Mason and I would arrive there at just about the same time.

And I was right. He was waiting at the turnoff to Dog Hollow Road when we got there. There was a trailer on the corner, and not much but farm fields everywhere else. I gave him a wave, and drove on by, up the hill and into oblivion.

"There," Natalia said a few miles later. Interestingly, she said it just as we approached the brown and yellow wooden Dog Hollow State Forest sign. But whatever. I pulled over and my faithful cop pulled over right behind me. Gravel crunched under my tires. I got out and took a lungful of the fresh, pine-and-sunshine-scented air. Should've left the top down. It was such a great day. I should be out on the lake with the kids and the dogs, not up here keeping a phony psychic out of Chief Cantone's Beyoncé hair.

Yes, I was as jealous of the chief's hair as I was of her eyebrows. And don't even get me started on her boobs.

"There's a trailhead," I said, pointing. "Why don't we start there? You can lead the way, Natalia."

Nodding, but not speaking, she hurried to hop across the ditch, and started up the well-worn path into the woods. It wasn't too terribly steep, but it did angle upward from the road and I wasn't sure whether Natalia was up to it. She surprised me though, taking off at a quick and steady clip in her very cool boots. I started to follow, but Mason touched my arm, and gave me a "hold up a second" look.

I waited until Natalia was out of sight, then longer, until her noisy footfalls were no longer audible. And then I said, "I know this is a waste of time. It wasn't my call. But you really didn't have to come all the way out here. You should be following real leads, Mason." I was glad he was with me–I was always blissful-bordering-on-stupid when he was close to me. I know, sickening. But he ought to be out searching for Josh's friend.

"You're that sure she's a fake?" He lifted his eyebrows when he asked me, and watched me with those intense cop-eyes of his that didn't miss a thing.

"Of course I am. There are no such things as psychics."

"Except for you, right?"

"I am Not—"

"I know. But you have *something*. And if you have it, then how can you be so sure no one else has it, too?"

I hated when he was logical. He thinks with his brain. I think with my gut. "I'm not sure *no one* else has it. I'm just sure *she* doesn't have it."

And then, like he always did, he took what I said right into him, accepted it without question. "Okay, I get that. And I trust that. But I need more. So what makes you so sure she doesn't have it, then? What's your evidence?"

"Oh, stop being such a cop. I just am, okay? I just feel it."

"Up here!" Natalia cried. "There's something up here!"

I closed my eyes. *Please don't let it be a body.*

We jumped the ditch and jogged up the trail. Natalia was standing just off the path, one hand pressed against a pine tree's trunk, blinking like a mole at high noon and looking around without really seeing. Like her focus was turned inward.

She held out her hands, closed her eyes, and started walking unsteadily deeper into the woods. Mason shot up beside her, grabbed her shoulders and said, "Go slow. I'll keep you from hitting anything."

"No need," she said, and she stopped walking. "It's right here. It's right here, there's something right–"

"Holy shit," I said, and when Mace shot a look my way, I pointed at the bright red Converse high top basketball sneaker not five feet ahead of where Natalia had stopped walking. And I knew in my bones it belonged to Hunter Marks.

Mason turned, saw it, and swore. "Nobody touch anything." Then he pulled out his phone and called it in.

CHAPTER 4

I sat on the floor in the giant living room of my unfinished, unoccupied, under-construction house, feeling self-conscious even though I was alone. The contractors kept saying they were winding down, wrapping up, almost done.

They'd better finish soon, or I was going to start moving in around them. To hell with patience. The camper was small, and as my favorite TV show reminds me often, winter is coming. The walls were still sheetrock and spackle. The hardwood floors were gorgeous, but covered in protective cloth and plastic, so you couldn't see them.

I sat in the middle of the floor, right below where the chandelier would be. At the moment, there was just a colorful tangle of wires sticking out of the ceiling above me. But never mind all that. I was here to focus.

I had my cell phone in front of me. True to her word, Natalia DaVine had texted me her "process" and like an idiot who watched *Ancient Aliens* religiously (which I did) and believed every word of every episode (which I did not), I was going to try it.

I read through the process first, just to know what to expect. "This is totally stupid," I said.

Then don't do it, said my Inner Bitch.

"I have to try."

Because...?

"Because it's so stupid it just might work," I told her in my best TV detective tone.

So I sat there, relaxed my body, and took deep breaths. Natalia might be a phony baloney bullshit fraud, but I wasn't much better at the moment. The only signal my antenna was still pulling in was the one that alerted me whenever Mason got that randy feeling in his jeans. And I think I'd pick that up even if I was in a coma.

I was at the point where I would try anything to get my NFP back. I needed to help find Hunter. The poor damn kid was abducted, bleeding, and missing a sneaker. He needed me.

I glanced at Natalia's text and re-read the first line.

"'Visualize a spiral staircase that descends down into the earth.'"

Right. How the hell does a spiral staircase descend into the earth? I guess the stairs could sort of line the outside of a big hole, right? Twisting downward, with the middle part open?

I tried that, but the hole was too wide, so I tried making it smaller and looked at the text again.

"The top step is red. And then the next step is orange. The third step is yellow. The fourth is green. As you stand on each stair, imagine the color bleeding up into you. It colors your shoes, your legs, your gown."

My *gown?* I was barefoot and wearing jeans. I tried imagining the stair color dying my skin and my clothes. The dirt from the sides kept spilling onto the steps and muddying up the color, though.

I hadn't got very far down my staircase. Glancing at the text, I saw she had only given me seven steps. Which was really stupid. You could barely make one decent loop with seven steps, much less an entire spiral staircase.

I imagined myself back at the top, and this time I tried making the first seven steps red, and imagined myself walking down them. I made the next seven steps orange, and decided this wasn't so bad, or so hard, but there was no way it was going to work. I stepped down onto the yellow flight, and then onto the green. I giggled a little imagining my face and hair turning green. *I'll get you, my pretty!*

Damn, I'm funny.

Three flights to go. Blue, then indigo, which was just another word for blue, which pissed me off so much I almost trashed the whole thing. Why didn't she just say light blue and dark blue? If I hadn't been so close to the end, I would have quit right then.

Finally, I was on the last set of stairs, which were purple. And still nothing. It wasn't going to work. I was still pissed about "indigo" as I counted my way slowly down seven purple steps.

I was pretty deep into my earth hole by then. I sat down on the bottom step, closed my eyes, and decided to imagine a crystal cave like I'd seen on the Discovery Channel, and BAM! I sort of exploded out of my body through the top of my head, and landed somewhere else.

I was a boy with one shoe, and I was running through the woods. My heart was pounding so hard I could hear it in my ears. Someone was chasing me. My knee was bleeding through a tear in my jeans. It was dark outside. The person chasing me got closer. I heard him crashing through brush and it was getting louder, and I turned to look back over my shoulder while still running forward. The next thing I knew, I was falling backwards, and my heart was in my throat.

I hit the ground hard, far below. The air gusted out of my lungs and my head cracked against a boulder. Pain shot all the way to my fingers and toes. And then I just lay there, blinking and staring up above me.

The night sky was beautiful. Clear and dark, dark blue. Indigo, right? And all those stars just winking and twinkling. There was a stream bubbling and tumbling past me, only a few feet away. I wanted to turn to look at it, but I couldn't seem to move.

Something rustled up above. It was the man, standing

at the edge I'd fallen from. I didn't know if he could see me. I told myself to lie really, really still, and then almost smiled, because I couldn't move anyway. I couldn't move if I tried.

He looked right where I was. I closed my eyes and prayed it was too dark for him to see me.

There was a whoosh, and my eyes popped open, and I was back inside my own body, looking up at my own ceiling. I was lying on my back on the floor of my unfinished living room, blinking up at the wires sticking out where the chandelier would be.

And then I sat up fast. "It worked. I can't believe that fake, wanna-be psychic's bullshit process actually worked."

Maybe she wasn't such a phony after all.

I scrambled to my feet, picked up my phone, and tapped my man's gorgeous face with my thumb. He answered on ring number one. "Hey babe. What's up?"

I warmed at the endearment and tried not to tingle. This was no time for tingling. "Hunter was being chased through the woods. He fell over a cliff, into a ravine, and hit his head on a rock. I think he's hurt."

"It's back? Your...stuff?"

"Yes, apparently my stuff is back. But that's not the headline here. Where are you?"

"Searching Dog Hollow. Natalia called a half hour ago. She had a vision, too. Described an abandoned hunting cabin where she says the kid's being held. Police chopper spotted the place from the air. Matches her description to a T. I'm leading a team up there now."

"Okay, but he's not there. He's lying on his back at the bottom of a ravine with a creek running past him. At least he was."

"She says he's in the cabin"

"Well, how long before you get there and prove her wrong?"

I could almost see him smirking at me.

"An hour, maybe two. We're on foot. If he's not at the cabin, we'll follow your lead next. I'll call you back."

"Be careful, Mace. But he's not in there."

I hung up and headed outside and across the wide front lawn toward the camper, which I had loved at first and was rapidly growing to hate. Camping was fun. Being forced to live in a camper while paying way too much to a crew of men who worked at the pace of geriatric snails, was not. Josh and Jeremy were across our dirt road on the dock, fishing in the sprawling reservoir with Myrtle and Hugo snoozing contentedly at their feet. The moonlight on the water and the boys in silhouette was such a striking sight that I pulled out my phone and snapped a quick picture. I couldn't help myself. Beauty just stopped me in my tracks. Side effect of being blind for most of my life. Go figure.

"Hey guys. Want to help me find Hunter?"

Josh dropped his pole onto the dock, jumped to his feet and turned to face me all at once. Myrtle did likewise.

She was Josh's little shadow. "'Bout time!" Josh said. "Where we going?"

"Same patch of woods your uncle Mason and every cop in three counties is searching. Just a slightly different part of it."

"You finally have a vision, Aunt Rache?" Jeremy asked. The older, more responsible one, he picked up the fishing poles and tackle box, and brought them with him. Hugo trotted along nipping at Jere's shoelaces.

"Yes. Finally. He's near a stream, and he's hurt." It hit me again that Natalia DaVine's screwed up process had worked, which meant I was going to have to give some more thought to her validity. Even though she was dead wrong about Hunter being in some hunting shack. But I couldn't worry about any of that right then. We had to move. I felt it right to my toes. "We need to take the four-wheelers. It'll be faster."

We owned four Yamaha Grizzlies, one for each of us, because I believe in spoiling the people I love, and that includes me.

Oh, that was good! Note to self, "Spoil yourself the way you spoil your family." Great one-liner for the next book.

The ATVs were still on the trailer from our last adventure. "We'll have to take the Subaru," I said.

"I'll hook up the trailer." Jeremy leaned the fishing poles against the camper, scooped up Hugo and handed him to Josh.

"I'll put the dogs in," Joshua said, and he patted his thigh and went in to the camper with Myrtle on his heels.

"I'll get the map," I said. "And some shoes!" I headed to the T-bird for that handy-dandy atlas. Chalk up another one for Natalia DaVine, who'd bought the thing and then left it in my car. I tore out the page in question, folded it and stuffed it into my pocket.

The moon was an hour higher in the sky by the time we got there. Jeremy was backing three of the Grizzlies off the trailer, one at a time. We'd parked at the dead-end of the forest's public access road, about 750 feet from where a creek cut right through the woods. According to my map, there were four small creeks that crisscrossed the forest. None of them were named, but I'd have bet my right arm any local farmer would know what they were called. The longest creek was also the closest to the access road. We figured we'd follow it first, then if we didn't find anything, we'd move on to the next.

"You worried about leaving that one unattended?" Jeremy asked, with a nod at the fourth ATV, still on the trailer.

"Hell, no. I've got the keys and the woods are crawling with cops." I hopped on my ATV. "Let's go."

The three of us rolled out, headlights blazing, huge flashlights cradled between our thighs. I put my helmet on, because it was a good example for the boys. If I'd been alone, I would not have worn one. If I caught them riding without one, I'd kick their teenage asses. Yes, I'm a hypocrite. Sue me.

Driving carefully over ruts, around brush and briars, and under low hanging limbs, I led the way to the creek, and found it despite the darkness, right where the map said it should be. We stopped, and Jeremy looked up and down the bubbling stream, then at me. "Which way?" He had to yell to make me hear him over the low rumble of our machines.

I didn't have time to count my way down a set of multicolored imaginary stairs just then, so I went with my gut. "That way."

We rode, following the creek upstream, and it was beautiful, truly. Not a trail, just wilderness, untamed and messy. We had to pick our way around brush and boulders and toppled trees. Sometimes we had to drive in the water itself where it was shallow enough, just to make our way past the dense undergrowth that lined the banks.

I breathed the fresh air and kept my eyes peeled for any sign of a high spot from which Hunter could've fallen. Our headlights cut a wide swath, and we drove slowly enough to let us swing our flashlights around too, to see the moonlight dappled terrain off to either side of us.

And then I spotted it, a tall, steep rise off to my left, and I stopped my machine. The boys, who were behind me, stopped too, and I cut the motor and signaled them to do likewise. I tugged off my helmet and got up, moving the beam of my flashlight around the ground between the creek and the drop-off, and tried to recall the details of my vision and figure out where Hunter would be.

The boys wandered off in different directions, calling his name. It felt like he was close. Maybe a little further to the....

"Here! Over here!" Joshua yelled.

I ran his way and found him kneeling beside Hunter Marks, clasping his shoulders and yelling "Hunter! Hunter!" into the kid's still, pale face.

CHAPTER 5

Hunter Marks was only wearing one shoe.

That was the image seared into my stubborn brain as I paced the soles off my shoes in the waiting room of the Cortland Regional ER; that poor kid, lying on the mossy ground with a sneaker on one foot and a torn up, dirty sock on the other. He'd put some mileage on that sock, running through the woods of Dog Hollow.

Joshua was sitting near a window, his eyes wider than they ought to be. Jeremy was right beside him. We'd driven straight there from the scene, trailer, ATVs and all, just as soon as a helicopter had taken Hunter out of there. Mason was talking to the parents, who'd just arrived. I stopped pacing to watch him doing that thing he was so good at doing. A comforting hand on a mother's shoulder, an honest look into a father's eyes. He was good, he was so good. I wondered sometimes–okay, all the time–how I got so damn lucky to end up with a guy like him. I mean, I'm okay, but I'm not good like that. I don't know if you've noticed, but I can be kind of a bitch.

You don't say!

Right then, he looked up, like he could feel my eyes on him. And when they locked onto mine, I knew everything he was saying with those eyes of his. *Nice job finding the kid. I'm really glad you got your NFP up and running. Everything's gonna be okay. And by the way, I love you.*

Yeah. I'd sure as hell hit the jackpot. I tried to convey a reply, but a couple of doctors came out of the treatment room, so we all converged on them. Joshua squeezed up close to my side, and I put my arm around his shoulders, and had to reach up a little bit to do it. Mason stood beside Chelsea. Marks, and Jeremy, beside her husband.

Look at that kid, I thought. Tall and handsome and planning to be a cop just like his uncle. Jeremy was already stepping up.

"He's still unconscious," said a doctor who looked like she belonged on a magazine cover. Her name tag said Dr. Sumner. "But there's no sign of a head injury and his other injuries are minor."

The second doctor, young and handsome, and probably still in some phase of training, added, "He broke his wrist when he fell. Has a lot of cuts and bruises–"

"Then why isn't he awake?" Hunter's mother asked.

"We don't know," Dr. Sumner said. "But we're running

some tests to find out. My best guess is that he has some kind of sedative in his system that–"

"You mean he's been drugged?" Chelsea sent a terrified look at her husband.

"It's possible, but his vitals are strong. I have no reason to think–"

"Was he...is there any sign..." The mother's lips trembled, and she squeezed her eyes tight.

"What did that animal do to our son?" her husband asked.

Young Dr. Neely blurted, "As far as we can see, nothing."

"Wait, what?" I asked. "He wasn't–"

"There is no sign of sexual assault," Dr. Sumner said. "Of course, we'll know more when he–"

"Doctors, he's coming around," a nurse a few feet away said. She was holding open the door to Hunter's room.

The parents lunged for the door. So did Mason. I grabbed his arm though, and he stopped, met my eyes, nodded. The two docs headed into the room at the end of the hall, and the parents hovered nervously right outside the door that had been closed on them.

"I don't get it," I said to Mason.

He said, "I've got to get in there and talk to him. And I can't be too patient about it. We have a child predator on the lose."

At the word "predator" I flashed back to the vision I'd

had when I'd done that mental ride-along inside Hunter's head. He'd been lying on his back on the ground, looking up at the guy he'd been running from. And I had seen the guy through his eyes. I grabbed hold of the image, locked onto it, closed my eyes as if it might leak out otherwise, and said, "I saw him."

"You saw him," Mason repeated. Then his brows arched so high they made me want a Big Mac. "The kidnapper?"

"Yeah."

He clasped the back of my head, kissed me hard. "You're amazing, you know that?"

"Better than Natalia DaVine, right? Where is she, anyway?"

"Chief had a uniform drive her back to her hotel. She was pretty upset at the cabin."

"Because she was wrong?"

"Oh, she wasn't wrong. I'm pretty sure Hunter was in that cabin at some point. Place was a mess. Duct tape, a broken chair, scraps from a few meals—PB&J and root beer. A broken plate." He was tapping his cell, and I looked over his shoulder to see the recipient was Chief Cantone.

"Rachel got a look at suspect. Sketch artist?"

The reply was almost instant. "I'll get one. Give me an hour. Hunter?"

"Just regained consciousness. Parents with him. I'm next."

"Good."

He pocketed the phone, turned to the boys. "Jere, Josh, I need you to wait out here while Rachel and I talk to Hunter."

"Okay," Jeremy said.

"I want to see him, too." Josh hadn't stopped staring at the closed door since Hunter's parents had gone inside.

"I'll see if I can get you in, Josh." Mason clapped a scrawny shoulder. "You did good, you know."

"It was Aunt Rache," he said, adding in a stage whisper, "She got her stuff back."

"You're the one who spotted him, Josh," I said.

Jeremy nodded his agreement. "Guess detective genes just run in the family."

Josh smiled a little. Not much, but a little.

I dug around in my bag and found a handful of singles. "Why don't you guys raid the snack machine?"

Josh took the cash and the two of them headed off in search of places to spend it. Mason took my hand. "You okay?"

"Yeah. Sure, I'm good." He was walking toward Hunter's hospital room, pulling me right along beside him. "Uh...his parents aren't gonna want me in there, Mace."

"If it wasn't for you, we might not have found him for days."

"Yeah, but they don't know that. And they can't. We go public with this stuff I do and it'll ruin us. The kids. The gossip. Your job. The public. Just...no."

He nodded slowly. "I know you're right."

"I'm always right."

"You saw the guy, yeah?"

"Yeah. From inside Hunter's head."

"Then Hunter saw him, too."

"He must have."

Mason nodded, sent a rapid-fire text, then pocketed the phone and tapped on the door.

"What was that?" I asked, nodding at the pocket that held his phone.

"Told the chief to send the sketch artist to us. Hunter can help, too."

Then he opened the door and stuck his head in. "I know it stinks, folks, but it's important that Hunter and I talk while all this is fresh in his mind."

Apparently, the docs and parents agreed, because he went the rest of the way inside, and since he was still holding my hand, I went too.

Hunter lay in the bed looking pale and shaky. He was bigger than Josh, not taller, but more filled out. He had a head of shaggy yellow and brown hair and a cast on his forearm, wrapped around his hand like a fingerless glove. His mother sat on the bed beside him, and had a death grip on his other hand. His dad stood close beside her, looking like he didn't know what to say or do. Dr. Neely left before the door swung shut behind us. Dr. Sumner was still standing by the machines, looking at their drips and beeps and digital screens.

"Would it be all right with you all if I talk to Hunter alone for a few minutes?" Mason asked.

Chelsea Marks shot her husband a worried look.

I said, "It's easier to be completely open when you're not worried about upsetting your parents. Am I right, Hunter?" I sent him an encouraging smile.

He nodded, but I don't think it meant anything. His parents left, his mom hugging him gently. She didn't want to let go, and I didn't blame her.

When we were alone with the kid, I wandered to the window and looked outside. I needed my eyes on something else so I could listen with my other senses. There were a handful of reporters out there. I was glad someone had kept them from taking over the waiting room.

Mason sat down in the chair near the bed, and said, "How're you doing, Hunter?"

"Better now," he said.

"I'll bet. Must've been the scariest thing that ever happened to you, huh? I know Josh was pretty scared when it happened to him."

Hunter responded to that. I felt him respond to it.

"He's the one who found you, you know."

"Really?"

"Yeah. He'd like to visit you when we finish up, if the docs say it's okay."

"Cool."

"So...can you tell me what happened? I know you were riding your bike home from the fair...."

"Yeah. I was almost there, too. Guy hit me with his car. I went flying into the ditch. I thought it was an accident at first. Then he came over, I thought to help or see if I was okay or whatever. But he just grabbed me and threw me in his car." He shook his head as if he still couldn't believe it.

"Car, huh? You remember what color?"

"It was white." Hunter nodded. "It was plain looking."

"But it was a car, not an SUV or a crossover..."

"Car. Four-door. Rust around the wheel wells. I grabbed onto one of them when he was trying to shove me in, and it broke right off."

Behind my closed eyes, I saw it happen, felt the rusty metal cutting into the creases of his fingers. And the terror. Poor kid.

"Okay. Got it. You're doing great."

"He stuck me with a needle. Knocked me out," Hunter went on. "When I woke up again, I was in some kind of hunting shack. I don't even know where."

"In the woods out by Cuyler," Mason said.

"He kept me tied up...well, taped me up. He'd cut my hands loose so I could eat and use the toilet, but then he'd tape me right back up again. He wore a mask the whole time. A Scooby-doo mask."

Mason said, "This is a really hard question to ask, Hunter, but it's important. Did he do anything to you? Sexual stuff?"

"No. No sex stuff, no kid porn stuff, nothing like what you see on TV. He didn't do anything to me. Just kept me taped up and kept telling me I'd get to go home soon, and not to worry, that nothing bad was going to happen to me."

Mason glanced my way. I sensed it, and looked back, gave him a nod. Hunter was telling the truth. I could hear a lie the way Myrtla can hear me open the fridge.

"How'd you get away?" Mason asked.

"I figured I was dead if I didn't. The last time he untied me to eat, I broke the plate, slashed him with it, and ran like hell. He chased me. I guess I fell or something. I don't remember."

"Yeah, you fell. So, you never saw his face?"

"No. I don't think so."

I turned away from the window. "When we found you, you were lying at the bottom of a ravine, face up," I told him. "Are you sure you didn't see him standing at the top when you first landed, maybe looking down at you?"

He frowned, and then his brows rose and he blinked. "Yeah. That's right, I did. I was thinking I had to stay really still so he wouldn't see me."

"But you could see him," I said.

He nodded. "How did you know?"

I shrugged. "I'm a good guesser."

"You just keep what you saw in your mind, kiddo," Mason said. "We have a police sketch artist coming over to get your description. Now, was there anything else?"

He shook his head.

Mason said, "When did you lose your shoe?"

Hunter blinked and said, "I didn't lose it. That weirdo took it. Just took it right off my foot and left me there."

"He took your shoe?"

"Yeah. The freak."

Mason and I exchanged a look.

Hunter said, "Mr. Brown, you're gonna catch him, right?"

"You better believe I am," Mason said. "And I'm gonna make sure you're safe until I do."

The kid looked only mildly reassured. And then he said, "Can Josh come in now?"

"I'll go get him," I said. I didn't have to go far. When I opened the door, Josh was waiting on the other side. I held the door for him, and then Mason and I stepped into the hallway.

"What the hell do you make of that whole thing with the shoe?" I asked.

"I don't know," he said. "But I'm damn well planning to find out."

CHAPTER 6

I stood in a quiet corner of the small hospital's large, comfortable waiting room, pretending to look out the window with my eyes closed. If anyone noticed, I didn't know or care.

Mason was talking to Hunter's parents again, and waiting for the sketch artist to show up. Josh was in Hunter's hospital room visiting his friend. Jeremy slouched in one of the chairs as if he'd melted there, his long legs akimbo—that's a thing, right? He was texting someone, probably Misty, who was both my niece and his girlfriend. And the waiting area was empty aside from us. So I just meandered over to the most secluded corner of the waiting room, despite its windows, and closed my eyes and tried to tune in to Josh, in Hunter's room.

I didn't even know if it would work. I couldn't usually

tap into someone at will. But Josh and I had become really close lately, and I just had a feeling...he needed me in there with him.

"It's okay if you want to cry," Josh said.

Just like that I was there, doing a ride-along in his sweet head. I heard his voice through his own ears, and felt him frantically searching his brain to find the right thing to say. A thing that would help his friend. I wondered if I could send him suggestions.

"At least with you, it was your mom," Hunter said.

Josh shook his head. "I don't know if that makes it better, man. I spent the whole time afraid she was gonna kill me."

"I was pretty sure my guy was gonna kill me, too," Hunter said.

"I think it's worse thinking your own mom might kill you than thinking a stranger might kill you."

"No way. It was your *mom*. You had to know deep down your own mom wasn't gonna kill you, no matter how crazy she is."

"Dude!"

"Sorry." Hunter lowered his head. He was sitting up in the bed, and I guessed Josh had probably raised it for him. Or maybe he'd done it himself. If a kid could figure out video games, he could probably figure out how to raise a hospital bed.

Then Hunter peered up at Josh, a grin on his face. "It's

probably funny, us arguing over who had the worst kidnapping."

I felt Josh's mood lift. "It is pretty funny." They smiled at each other for a minute. Josh thought it felt just like old times. "You're gonna be okay, though."

"You think?"

"I was. Am, I mean." Josh thought for a long beat. He didn't need any suggestions from me. He was doing just fine.

I felt him remembering, a flash that came so fast I couldn't translate it all, if that makes any sense. He could, though. It was his thought, after all. Just like a native could cut loose a rapid-fire string of words in his own tongue, and know exactly what he meant, but a kid who'd taken three years of his language in high school wouldn't have a clue. Translating someone else's thoughts is just like that.

It didn't matter though, because Josh repeated it all in words, to his pal. "You might be more scared than you used to be. I mean, you were probably never scared at all. But you might be now. The worst is when you dream it. You wake up just sure you're still there, and it takes a minute before you figure out you're in your own room, in your own bed."

"That happen a lot, Josh?"

Josh nodded. "It's getting less, though. I think that means it'll go away after a while."

"All right." Hunter seemed to think about that, and every few seconds he nodded slow. Then he looked Josh in the eyes and said, "What else?"

Josh shrugged. He was getting very uncomfortable talking about this, but he also thought it was helping Hunter. And that's what he wanted to do. So he made himself keep going.

"Sometimes you might think you see her—him, I mean."

"See him?"

"Like around a corner, or off in the shadows, or mixed in with a bunch of other people. But then you look closer and there's no one there."

My heart was breaking for my sweet Joshua.

"That sounds damn creepy," Hunter said.

"It is."

"Is that getting less, too?"

"Not really. It might just be because it was my mom, though. Part of me wants to see her."

"Even after all she did?"

Josh nodded. "She's my mom."

"You're right, dude. Yours was way worse."

"Maybe. I didn't fall off a cliff and end up in the hospital, so...."

Hunter laughed a little, then held up a fist. "Call it a tie?"

Nodding, Josh fist-bumped him. Then he screwed up

his courage to say just a little bit more, because he thought he should. "Maybe it won't work the same with you. But if it does, or something different happens, you can tell me about it. I'll get it. And I won't tell anyone else."

"If you did, I'd thump you."

"I never told anyone else about mine," he said.

"I won't either," Hunter promised.

I felt guilty for listening in, and I tuned out right then, opening my eyes, focusing on everything around me. The room, the chairs, the floor. Mason over near the big entrance, and Chief Gorgeous Cantone, shaking her bon-bon closer to the doors.

I loved Vanessa. I did. If she'd been hetero, I'd have probably detested her, because she had the body of a sex goddess and I envied it. Her skin was naturally the tone some women spend hours in a tanning booth for. She had dark, smoky eyes and dark silky hair. If she was straight, I'd be jealous of Mason spending so much time working with her. But she was happily married and raising a little girl with her wife, and that was fine with me.

She was accompanied by a scrawny man with too much oil in the few whips of blond hair that were combed back-to-front, over his baldness. He wore round black-rimmed glasses. You know, the kind worn by the evil scientist in every sci-fi flick.

The doors opened, and I headed over to meet them. Jeremy got up and came with me, and we shared an encouraging look with each other. Mine was the one I would give to a kid to reassure him. His was the one a strong, capable police officer would give to a crime victim. Already. He was gonna be a great cop someday.

Vanessa smiled at me, reached a hand out to clasp my shoulder instead of doing the manly handshake thing. She was comfortable in her job. She didn't try to emulate maleness to keep it. She let her sexy shine, unapologetically. I admired that about her.

"Hey, Rachel," she said. "This is our sketch artist, Rohan Blett."

Blett, I could believe. But Rohan? Seriously?

"Rohan, this is Detective Mason Brown and Rachel de Luca. Rachel is a department consultant who also might've got a look at our suspect."

I nodded hello as Mason moved closer to me, his eyes giving me the once-over before moving to meet Rohan's. "Good to meet you. Let's get you in to see Hunter."

I put my hand on his arm. "I think we should give Hunter a little more time with Josh."

Mason looked at me, frowned a little. I gave a nod with my eyes. The kind where I don't move my head at all, but he still knows what I'm saying. Either he was NFP too, or we were spending way too much time together.

Not.

"Why don't we do my sketch first?" I suggested.

"Good idea," Vanessa said. "I'll see if they can find us a room to use."

M y session with Rohan, the Sketch Man, took about an hour. I told him everything I could remember, and the resulting image looked nothing like what I saw in my mind.

I looked at it and I knew it was exactly what I'd seen with my eyes, and that it matched every way I'd tried to describe to the artist. And yet in my mind, I'd *felt* the kidnapper. I felt him clearly, his energy. It was aggressive, but it was also frantic. I would know him if I saw him again, but not by his face. And there was no way to draw that. No way to tell anyone else how to recognize it.

"I should see the boy now," Rohan said.

"Give me one minute," Mason replied. Then he put his arm around my shoulders and steered me outside. We walked across the parking lot, out toward the SUV with the trailer still attached and the four-wheelers still onboard. Then he turned me toward him and pulled me close. Just wrapped his arms around me and held me there, against him. I could hear his heart beating underneath my ear. I closed my eyes, and just basked in him for a second.

"It was traumatic for you, finding Hunter out there like that. Are you sure you're okay?"

"I am," I said. "Josh isn't, though."

He clasped my shoulders and set me back, so he could

see my face, search my eyes, read the open book I was to him. "Tell me."

"I only meant to check in on him and Hunter just now. Wasn't even sure I could do it. I can't usually just tap into someone at will, but Josh and I are so close, I thought maybe—"

"That's amazing," he said. "I love you for that. So?"

"He was talking about flashbacks, nightmares, waking up thinking he's still there, in that cabin where his mother held him. Seeing her everywhere. And it's tearing him up, because part of him wants to see her."

He nodded. "Then he needs to see her." He said it in an unmistakable and-I'm-gonna-make-it-happen way.

"But her doctors thought it would be bad for her."

"Not seeing her will be bad for the kids. On a good day, I think she'd agree with me that it's worth the risk."

I nodded. He was right. "I think Josh might need to talk to someone. You know, a therapist, grief counselor, something."

"Okay. I'll bring it up with the department shrink, get some recommendations."

I loved that he listened to me. He didn't question that I'd somehow tapped into a conversation happening three rooms away, or doubt my opinion on what Joshua needed. That kind of trust in me, confidence in me, pure unadulterated belief in me, just blew me away, and not for the first time.

"Have I told you lately how amazing you are?" he

asked. He had both hands on my shoulders, the length of his arms between us. "Or how damn lucky we three Brown guys are to have you? Or how much we love you?"

"Not lately enough." I went in for the kiss, twined my arms around his neck and stood on tiptoe to get a little more of him. "And right back at you."

"Shower me in praise, why don't you?"

I grinned. Have I mentioned I think I slipped and landed in a big steaming pile of paradise? "Josh is gonna be okay. And you should be proud, Mason. He really helped Hunter in there." I tilted my head. "Your nephews are as wonderful as you are, you know that?"

He gave me a smile and the dimple of doom tickled my tickle receptors. Big time. "That's more like it." He kissed me once more, then turned me, still holding me tight to his side, and we started back toward the ER doors. "Sketch thing didn't work out very well, did it?"

"I felt like I got a better look at him than that," I said. "And I did, but not with my eyes, you know?"

"No, I have no idea."

"I'll know him if I see him," I said.

He nodded. "Take the boys home, if you want. I'll grab some takeout when I come. We'll have a good night, celebrate that Hunter's safe."

I nodded. "I'm in. What about Rohan the Magnificent?"

He sent me a sideways look of amused disapproval.

"I'll stay until Hunter's sketch is done and then I'll be home."

I looked up fast. "What about Hunter? There's a kidnapper out there who thinks the only person who might be able to ID him is in that hospital."

"We're leaving officers to watch Hunter's room. He'll be safe."

"How long is the department going to be willing to spring for that?" I asked in full-blown cynic-mode.

"Not long. So I've gotta find some suspects for you to look at fast."

We opened the doors to head inside, saw Vanessa and Rohan in the hallway outside Josh's room. I leaned into Mason's side and said, "It's all about that sneaker. I just know it is."

Mason nodded. "Would it help to have it? Touch it?"

"Does my bulldog fart when she sits down?" He grinned at the image. I ignored it and rushed on. "Hell, yes, it would help. But how am I gonna do that? It's evidence, isn't it?"

He seemed to be thinking. "Can you feel through plastic?" he asked.

I knew he was talking about the evidence bag in which Hunter's shoe was currently sealed. "I don't know. I could sure try."

He nodded slowly. "I might be a little later getting home than I thought. I forgot something at work." Then he winked.

I wasn't about to tell him not to do what I knew he was going to do. We had a child abductor to catch. I slid my hand inside his, threaded fingers, gave a squeeze. Then we went into Hunter's room to draw stick figures with Rohan Bletts.

CHAPTER 7

The boys and I were inside our house, doing yet another walk-through after yet another day of reconstruction. Myrtle was walking around sniffing everything, clearly puzzled and irritated. Sure, this was her home, but everything was different, everything had changed. Every familiar smell had been burned away and now there were all new ones to learn.

"This is really starting to come together, isn't it?" I asked no one in particular. The living room had a hardwood floor, painted walls, trim all in place, and tangled wires with caps on their ends where the light fixtures would be.

Jeremy nodded. "It's been like, nothing, nothing, nothing, bam! Progress all at once."

"There's a sink!" Josh yelled. Then, "And the faucets work!"

"Careful, Josh. We don't know if the drains do!" I ran out there, dogs on my heels, little Hugo snorting and snuffling all the way. It was so cute how he stopped and waited for Myrt to catch up before continuing to romp into the kitchen. I waited too, forcing down my excitement, but then hurrying her along once she took up position with her side pressed to my calf.

She looked up at me, blind eyes seeming to say, *Look, it's different and I'm blind. Give me a minute, will you?*

I crouched and scratched her head. "I'm sorry, old girl. You just take your sweet time."

Damn straight I will.

Yes, my bulldog swears at me. I am fairly certain I do not imagine my interpretations of her expressions so much as translate them into human speak.

We entered the kitchen together, and the double stainless-steel sink was right there, gorgeous and shiny, atop the brand new, still-doorless and topless cabinets. And there, leaning against a nearby wall, cardboard in the shape of what could only be....

"My new granite countertops," I whispered

"You think?" Jeremy asked.

"You're the future detective. Go look. Do it, I can't stand it."

Grinning, Jeremy walked his tall, lanky bod over to the box, fiddled around until he'd loosened up a corner, and then tore it back while I held my breath.

Veils of thin protective wrap entombed its contents.

"For fuck's sake—Pete's sake. I meant for Pete's sake." I attacked it with my otherwise harmless short nails. And then the wrapping finally gave way to the gleaming, polished black granite, and the gold flecks that permeated it. "Oh, it's beautiful. Better than I even imagined." I ran my hands over its smooth, cold surface, whispering, "My precious,"

Then I stood back and nodded at the boys hard. "Eh? Eh?"

"It's really sparkly, Aunt Rache," Josh said.

"It's absolutely you," Jeremy added.

Neither, I noted, said they liked it. "Do you hate it?" And then I realized I hadn't really asked their opinion when I'd ordered it. "I kind of bulled through the kitchen stuff without consulting the Brown part of the tribe, didn't I?"

"You were having so much fun," Jeremy said. "We consulted on it and decided we didn't care enough about kitchen details to rain on your parade."

"You consulted on it?"

He nodded. "Uncle Mace, Josh and me." Then he looked at the countertop again and said, "I do kind of like it, though."

"Knock, knock," Mason called from somewhere near the front door. "Anyone call for pizza?"

We met him halfway through the dining room, where he stopped to look around. "Is it just me or has there been sudden, massive progress?"

"It's not just you." I said, leaning past the pizza boxes to kiss him hard on the mouth. "My countertop is here. I'm deliriously happy and also very sorry I left you men out of the planning on that. But mostly deliriously happy."

"When you're happy, everybody's happy, Rache." He gave me a look that had the balls to suggest the opposite was also true. I pretended not to see it.

He set the pizzas on a scaffold's lowest level, and the boys descended. No paper plates, no nothing.

"You stain anything with tomato sauce, you die." I used my most menacing tone.

The boys grinned and headed right out the front door, pulling it closed behind them. Taking a seat on a covered spackle pail, I took a gooey slice and enjoyed a bite. Pizza is the perfect food. I don't care, it just is.

"Did you get it?" I asked in between nipping up a dangling string of mozzarella.

"I did." He nodded at the front door. He'd left a backpack on the floor just inside it. "You ready?"

"You wanna let me finish my pizza?"

He just smiled, gave me one of those slow nods of his.

I ate my pizza. He went and got the backpack, brought it to me. Then he grabbed the pizza box and headed outside.

I got up and lunged after him, snatching another slice before he made it to the door.

He just shook his head. "I love you, de Luca, you

freaking nut. Take your time. I'll keep the boys out of your hair."

Yeah, that was the look I loved. That you're-batshit-but-I-love-it look. "Thanks."

He shook his head. "We're nowhere near even."

"Get out of here before I…" I looked him up and down. "Mm, mm, mm."

"Shut up," he said, and then he headed out, blushing, the shit. Blushing. Damn, I loved that man.

I walked through the house, taking the backpack upstairs, where I found the master bedroom with everything complete except the carpet. Deep green, soothing walls. Maple wood trim. A set of French doors with a little balcony on the other side. I was gonna put a pair of chairs out there for Mason and me, so we could sit holding hands, and watch the sun come up over the reservoir.

Heaving a sigh, I wiped my hands clean, then unzipped the backpack and took out the latex gloves it held. I pulled them on, snapped them dramatically like a surgeon, and smiled at myself a little. "Here goes nothing."

I reached in and felt the plastic evidence bag that held Hunter's sneaker. I closed my hand around it, and a bolt of lightning struck me right between the eyes.

I was him! I was inside the head of the kidnapper. I had a big, male body. My pits were damp. I had a case of the shakes way down deep inside me, like a low-level hum, vibrating, making my heart go faster, making my stomach knot up.

I was in the woods, looking around, then looking at a map that had a star marked on it in green glitter ink.

In my hand, I carried a boy's basketball shoe with a few drops of blood on it. "This must be it," I/he said. And I knew, because he knew, that we weren't the ones who'd put that green glitter star on the map. We were just trying to match it up to a spot in the real world. As ordered.

We stopped and turned in a slow circle, leaves crunching under our feet, releasing wafts of autumn-scented air. We breathed it in. It was cool and musty and rich. I felt him thinking that he had really fucked things up. He should've taken one of the other kids. Not this one. This one was tough, already a man, inside his own head.

Then we found the spot. He looked off to the left, and I did, too, right through his eyes, like I was peering out from inside his brain. Like I was him, only not. I wasn't in control.

And then he tossed the shoe.

I saw the trees, all tall pines and one scrawny maple struggling to get to the light. I recognized that spot. That was precisely where Mason and I had found Hunter's shoe.

"Babe?"

I landed in me again, coming down so hard it felt like I'd been dropped from the ceiling. My eyes popped open. Mason was kneeling in front of me. It was pitch dark around us, so a lot more time had passed than I would've thought. He had a flashlight in one hand, aimed at the floor. "You all right?"

I nodded. "He planted the sneaker right where we found it. It was deliberate. Planned. He had a map showing exactly where to put it."

"This is good." Mason set the flashlight down, pulled his phone from his pocket and started tapping notes to himself. "This is good intel, Rache. What else?"

"He's working for someone else. Following orders. He's just kind of a... a henchman."

"A henchman? What're you, reading Mike Hammer novels again?"

I grinned. "I never stopped. The guy's a thug. A lacky. A drone."

"Now you're just showing off." He returned to tapping his phone. "Noted. Anything else?"

"I don't think he's too bright." I shrugged one shoulder. "That's it, that's everything I got."

"It's enough. It'll lead us to something, it has to." He took the bagged sneaker from my hand, slid it into the backpack and zipped it up. His prints on the evidence bag wouldn't matter. He'd found the shoe, bagged it, and taken it in. Mine, however, shouldn't be there.

I peeled off the gloves and shoved them down deep into a nearby trashcan full of busted up sheetrock. There were other gloves in there, spackle-covered, paint-spattered rubber gloves. "When are you taking it back to the evidence room?"

"Tonight. Fewer people around."

"You better not get your sweet ass caught," I said.

"I won't." He slung the backpack over his shoulder, gave me a big juicy kiss, and took off to head back to the PD with his borrowed evidence.

He never came back. Not all night long. I couldn't get him on the phone. I was getting nothing from him. No signal, no insight. No NFPism. It was different with Mason. Always had been.

So I lay awake in the camper and worried myself sick until 5 a.m., when the BPD finally got around to letting him make his phone call.

CHAPTER 8

Chief Vanessa Cantone and I ran into each other at the top of the stairs, right outside BPD's main entrance. She was wearing a light blue dress that hugged her all the way to her knees. Very respectable length. She'd classed it up with a cropped navy jacket, a bolero or whatever. Sue me for not knowing fashion. The shoes matched the jacket, navy pumps. Very put together, very professional and still sexy as sin. She couldn't seem to help it. She'd be sexy in a feedbag. Did men ever harass her? You bet your ass they did. Once. Only once per asshole, early in her career. Then word got around. She took them down, often painfully, and then she talked to their wives.

"Why the hell didn't he call me?" she asked, as she opened the door and held it.

I preceded her in. "Maybe he only got the one."

"Yeah, right." She said it sarcastically, like she thought I was joking. I wasn't.

She came up beside me and our shoes tapped down the hall in perfect synch. I wore leggings with tall brown boots and a swooshy paisley print top. I don't know why, but I'm always compelled to dress nicer than normal if I'm going to be with Vanessa. Competitive, I guess. And it had been as easy to pull on pretty things as not this morning, as I'd dressed to rush to my hunky detective's side.

"So, what do you know?" she asked.

I'd sent Vanessa a quick text on my way in. Yes, while driving. But I did wait until I was sitting at a red light, so I get credit for that.

"What do *you* know?" I countered. Because what the hell was I gonna say? That Mason got caught returning evidence to the evidence room?

She looked at me, pressed her way-plumper-than-mine lips, said nothing. We walked in silence until she pivoted around a corner and into what I took to be the evidence area. I'd never seen this part of the place before. There was a fellow at a desk, rugged looking, short but muscular, dark hair and an impressive 'stache. He got up as we entered, opened another door and led us through into a small room where Mason was. I met his eyes, mine conveying relief and worry all wadded up together. His eyes beamed confidence, or tried to. There was a little uncertainty behind it. Hell, he might be in real trouble here.

I told you not to get caught, I thought at him.

I almost thought he heard me, too, the way he gave me about a third of a crooked smile. Not enough to deploy the dimple, but just shy of that.

There was a long table with a couple of chairs, one of which Mason was occupying, or had been. He rose when we came in. There was a counter along one wall, coffee pot and a mini fridge, etc. It looked like a break room.

"What's going on?" Chief Cantone asked.

"Ask him," Mason said, nodding toward the uniformed man whose nameplate read Sgt. Santini.

So the chief turned her dark brown eyes to him.

Santini was not in a good mood. His scowl hadn't faltered since I'd set eyes on him. "I came in for my shift. Found Detective Brown in the evidence room, with my keys."

"Well, you weren't there," Mason said. "But your keys were, so—"

"What were you doing in the evidence room, Brown?" The chief sent a quick look my way, as if to suggest I knew the answer to that, and she knew I knew it.

"I was just standing there, waiting for Segeant Santini to arrive."

"For?"

"To double check that I'd booked everything in." His eyes slipped to mine to tell me again not to worry.

I said, "He's been forgetful lately. Probably just lack of sleep."

"Why did you have Santini's keys?" Vanessa asked.

I jumped in. Cause it's what I do. "A more pertinent question might be, why were Santini's keys there when he wasn't? You just, what, leave them lying around while you wander off for a smoke break?"

Santini pulled in his chin and shot a look at the chief. "Why is she even here?"

"She's with me," Mason said. "And it's not a bad question, she just asked. You know how important it is to preserve the chain of evidence."

That's right, baby, I thought. *Best defense is a good offense.*

Chief Cantone looked at the department's evidence custodian as if awaiting an answer. Santini, looking rather stunned at this turn of events, said, "I keep a spare set in my desk. Top drawer, always locked."

"Interesting that I found them on the floor, under the desk," Mason said. Then he looked at the chief. "That was so out of the ordinary that I went into the evidence locker to make sure he wasn't back there hog-tied or something."

"Hog-tied?" Santini asked. "Who the hell's gonna hog-tie me?"

"Some criminal who wants to get rid of the evidence we have on him," I said. "Obviously."

"We?" Santini delivered it with a helping of sarcasm.

"Yeah we. I'm a fucking consultant. Official and shit." I looked at Vanessa. "Do I need to get a lawyer?"

Vanessa looked at Mason, then at Santini. "Could the

keys possibly have fallen from the drawer without your knowledge?" She was staring hard at Santini, almost willing him to say yes and save her a pile of problems.

But I was looking at Mason, who was slightly behind her, out of her line of sight. He caught Santini's eye, and tipped his hand to his lips, like he was tipping up a bottle. Apparently, he'd found more in that locked desk drawer than the extra keys.

Santini stiffened. Vanessa picked up on the exchange and swung her head around, but Mason changed to rubbing his chin so quickly it was almost funny.

Then Santini said, "I guess I could have dropped them and not realized."

"All right, so next question," the chief said. "Did you see Detective Brown touch or tamper with any evidence?"

"No, Chief."

She shrugged. "So why did I get a pre-dawn phone call again? What exactly is it you thought I was going to do here?"

Santini pursed his lips. "Not a damn thing."

"Good." She jerked her head at Mason. "With me. Now."

He followed her out of the room. I linked my arm around his waist and walked close beside him.

We followed her back through the halls to the entrance, and then outside. When the doors closed behind us, Chief Cantone said, "What the hell was that about Mason?" Then she held up her hands. "Don't answer that. Just tell me, is it gonna compromise any investigation?"

"Not a chance."

She slanted a look at me, then back at him. "Go home. And stay there. Three days, no pay. I'll call it insubordination or something. It'll placate Santini."

"I didn't do anything to Santini."

"You invaded his space. That's his domain. I know damn well that story of yours was bullshit. You're just lucky he didn't catch you doing whatever you were really doing in there." She shook her head, rolled her eyes. "If this department didn't need you so damn bad, I'd fire your ass."

"I'll try to keep being essential, Chief." He closed his hand around mine, and we jogged down the steps to my car. His was parked somewhere, probably in the lot nearby or maybe the garage, but he didn't seem to care. He jumped into the passenger seat, and waved a calm goodbye to the chief as I pulled away from the curb and into traffic.

And then he lowered his head into his hands and muttered, "Holy crap, that was close."

We returned home, to our haven, even though it currently consisted of an unfinished shell and a camper on the front lawn. Mason was nervous. He wasn't a lawbreaker, as a rule. He'd always been one of the good guys. You know, aside from covering up that his dead brother had been a serial killer. Other than that, he was a Boy Scout.

"So, I've got free time," he said. "You?"

"Not so much," I said. "I'm having lunch with Natalia DaVine." I smiled at him. "Want to join us?"

"If I say I'd rather be shot, will you be mad?"

I looked at his sexy face and shook my head. "She's not all that bad. And I'm starting to think she might be for real. Her method worked like a charm to jumpstart my stalled NFP." I frowned, and said, "Maybe that's why I can't read her. Maybe people with, you know, stuff, can't read other people with stuff."

"You think?" he asked. He really wanted to know. I could tell.

"Damned if I know," I said.

So we headed home. We had a long, leisurely, heavy breakfast with the boys and the dogs. After breakfast we took turns in the camper's tiny shower. I thought about the great big tiled shower off my new–our new–master bedroom. Multiple heads, fog proof glass doors, heated floor tiles. Oh, yeah, that baby was gonna be a dream come true. I supposed I'd appreciate it more after being forced to use this one.

Then I re-dressed in the same clothes, only this time with a tank underneath the paisley top, because it kept sliding off one shoulder, and the tank would make it look deliberate. I added a little makeup and ran a brush through my hair, popped on some giant gold hoop earrings and thought I looked like a rerun of Sonny & Cher.

And I liked it.

Twenty years blind, and now with my vision restored, I was still, completely obsessed with bright colors and shiny baubles and beautiful things. I was pretty sure I always would be.

We walked and talked, and hung out together for a couple of hours, and then it was time for me to leave. Mason and the guys were going to visit Hunter in the hospital while I was out, so I had to drop them at the PD to pick up Mason's car.

From there I headed to the hotel where Natalia was staying, and went up to her room to knock on her door.

She opened it, wearing an orange and red patterned kaftan, with long purple and teal beads dangling. She seemed surprised to see me, though, and her suitcases were on the floor just inside.

"Did I get my dates mixed up?" I asked. "I thought we were having lunch today."

She blinked, then looked at the ceiling. "You are right, you are so right. I totally forgot. I'm sorry."

"You, um...you checking out?"

She glanced down at the bags, then back at me, and nodded. "Now that the boy is safe, there's really not much more I can do."

Well that didn't make sense to me at all. "The kidnapper is still at large," I pointed out. Not that she didn't already know that.

"You wouldn't know unless you've followed my career, but I've never been very good at solving these kidnappings. Just finding the kids in time."

"In time?"

"In time to save their lives," she said. Then she frowned. "How about you?"

"Me? What do you mean?"

"Oh, come on, Rachel, let's not kid each other. You have the gift." She opened the door wider. "Do you want to come in?"

I pursed my lips, looked inside, and said, "I was planning on food."

She smiled. "You have someplace in mind?"

"No one should come to Binghamton and not have spiedies."

"All right then," she said. "Let's do this. I'll grab my things."

She left the door wide open and walked back into her room. I lingered half-in, half-out, not wanting to be rude while she grabbed a handbag and a mustard yellow over-coat off the bed and re-emerged while tapping her cell phone. Then she smiled and tucked it back into her bag. "There. I put the driver off an hour. I'll still make the airport in plenty of time."

We swung by the front desk, and she dropped off her key and asked the desk clerk to send a bellman up for her bags. He tapped a few buttons and her bill printed out, and then he slid it across the desk to her.

She fumbled in her purse for a pen to sign the bottom, pulled one out at length, and then scrawled her name in green glitter ink.

CHAPTER 9

"Something wrong, Rachel?" Natalia asked in her sweet and motherly voice.

"No, I just...love your pen."

She pulled it back and looked at it, frowning, and then something dawned in her eyes. Her smile seemed extra sparkly when she pirouetted away from the desk and said, "I'm all yours, dear. You can pick my brain as much you need, to help you figure out your own gift."

My gift was telling me to get the fuck out of there. Because Natalia DaVine had a pen just like the one that had made the star on the map from my vision. And whoever had put that star on that map, had been the one giving orders to Hunter's kidnapper.

There was something else telling me to stick it out, though. This outing of ours was just lunch. I was driving. I would be in full control. Who knew what I might be able to learn? I led her out to my T-bird, and we got in. I had the hard top on today. It was fall, and it was starting to feel like it.

She got into Myrtle's seat and buckled up. "Have I told you how much I love your car?"

"Thanks. She's my baby."

"So where are we going for lunch?"

I started the engine, hit the phone button on my dash panel and had it dialing Mason before she had finished buckling her seatbelt. It was only when I said, "Hi, honey, I'm with Natalia," that she noticed what I'd done.

She turned, surprised, I think.

"Say hello to Mason, Natalia."

"Oh, um," she blinked at me, as if to ask WTF I was doing, but I just smiled like a sophomore and beamed at her.

"Hello, Mason."

"Hello, Natalia. I want to thank you again for your help. Even though Hunter wasn't where you thought he'd be, you helped us find valuable evidence. We're grateful."

"You're welcome." She nodded, almost humbly. "I wish I could do more."

"We're having lunch at the Spiedie Pit. Mason. And, before I forget, if you go to the store, see if you can find me a green glitter gel pen."

"A green glitter gel..."

"Gel pen. Natalia has one, and I'm so jealous."

There was a pause, just a beat longer than it should've

been. Then, "Okay, I'll check while we're out. See you soon, Rache. I love you."

"Love you, too." I tapped the red phone icon, sent Natalia a radiant smile, and wondered if either of us truly thought we were fooling the other. Me pretending I didn't know. Her pretending she didn't know I knew. "I love beautiful things, colors, sparkles. I think because I spent so much time blind."

"I see." She sounded sympathetic, and as I tried not to look at her, and pled with my weirdo supercharged intuition to read her, just this once, I started to wonder if she was buying my act, after all. Maybe she hadn't yet made the connection. Maybe she didn't remember she'd used the same gel pen to mark her henchman's map.

She had her phone out, was tapping away. I looked at her sharply just as she glanced up.

"Checking my flight," she said. "You can't depend on them staying on schedule these days."

"I hear that."

Suddenly, she yanked a small black revolver out of her handbag and pointed it at me. "Shall we stop playing now, Rachel?"

"I guess so," I replied, with a glance at the gun. "Be careful with that thing. Just tell me, what exactly do you want me to do?"

"Just drive."

"To where?"

"We'll take eighty-one. Northbound."

Closer to home. Yeah, not a bad idea. "Okay," I said.

So I drove. And as I drove, I inched my cellphone out of my jacket pocket, on the left, thank goodness. I didn't need to look at it. I knew where everything was. I'd memorized things like that for twenty years. It wasn't even all that hard. I slid my finger up the side to turn the sound off, then tapped the phone to wake it up and pressed in my thumbprint.

The upper left of the screen was where my Messages app sat. I tapped it, and then the spot where the microphone was and said, "Mason."

Natalia shot me a look, and I made damn sure I was staring at a car off in the distance when she did. And then I said, "No, it's not him." I tapped my thumb on the microphone symbol again as we approached the highway. "Eighty-one North you said?" I waited a second and then tapped Send.

"That's what I said."

I tapped the microphone again. "It's hard to drive when you're pointing a gun at me." I waited a beat, tapped Send again.

She lowered the barrel so it was aimed at the floor. "Better?"

"Yeah. Thanks."

"I didn't know they'd found Hank's map at the cabin."

"They didn't," I said.

She frowned. "Then how did you know about the pen? The green glitter gel pen?"

"Saw it," I said, tapping my head. "See, *my* bullshit's real. Unlike your bullshit which is just...bullshit."

"I can see you're a woman of class."

"Class, huh? So you have class? You think it's classy to kidnap little boys just to maintain your fraudulent rep as a psychic, you phony fucking scumbag?"

"Have you forgotten I have a gun in my hand?"

"Go ahead, use it, I'll ram us into the biggest tree I can find and take you out with me, you lying, cheating, child abusing waste of oxygen."

"I don't do any harm. We choose the strong kids, well-adjusted kids, even though the meek would be easier. We keep them tied up for a couple of days, safe and warm and well fed–"

"And terrified."

"And then I lead the police to where they're being held."

"After aging their parents about ten years apiece."

"They never get hurt."

"Hunter almost got killed."

"That was unintentional."

"Right. When you decided to kidnap little boys for a living, you never imagined one of them would get hurt, sooner or later. You didn't see that as inevitable."

"No, I didn't."

"Then I'll add idiot to your list of qualities."

She lifted the gun's barrel again. "Take the next exit."

I tapped the microphone icon and said, "Castle Creek?" Send. My fingers had better be in the right spots.

She narrowed her eyes at me, I inched my phone hand back up onto my lap and took the exit. This small town was where Mason's farmhouse used to be, before that crazy psycho stalker of his burned it to the ground.

Natalia guided me over two side roads I knew well, then told me to pull over.

Tap. "Behind that yellow pickup truck?" Send.

She frowned at me. The jig was up.

Tap. "NY plate 5b-7234." Send.

The barrel was pressing into my skull as she yanked my left arm around. I tried to keep the car from wiping out, and managed to bring it to a stop in a cloud of dust on the shoulder. But she managed to wrestle my cell phone from my hand. I couldn't really fight her all that hard, with a gun to my head.

She glared at me and all but spat the words, "Get. Out."

I got out, waved a hand in front of me to clear the dust, and saw the pickup about a foot from my bumper. Damn good thing she hadn't made me bang up my ride. I'd have killed her for that.

And then I felt him. The guy I'd sensed, seen, *been*, really. The kidnapper. I felt him even before he got out of the pickup and came at me. I'd have kicked him square in the balls if that bitch hadn't still been pointing her gun at me.

She shoved my cell phone into her handbag. "Get her into the truck, Hank. We need to get out of here and find another vehicle. She just told Detective Brown all about this one."

Nodding, he climbed behind the wheel. He was bigger in person. Big and silent and scary.

Natalia poked me with her gun until I got into the front seat, where I sat mashed between them while he drove and drove. He took back roads I was unfamiliar with, and eventually emerged into a populated area where we spotted a car with its keys still dangling from the switch. It was parked in front of an isolated house that appeared to have no one at home.

Hank started to get out, and she said, "Hank, no. I'm going take her in the new car. I want you to dump the truck."

"Where?"

"The sign we just passed said Jackson's Pond, ten miles, didn't it?"

He nodded.

"Take it there, find an isolated spot, and drive it right into the water. Make sure it sinks all the way down. Give me your cellphone."

He did, and she yanked its battery and tossed it into the woods. "This would connect you to that kidnapping." She took another phone, a burner, I assumed, out of the glove compartment, and handed it to him. "Use this one.

Call me as soon as you've dumped the truck, and I'll come pick you up."

He took the new phone, obeying her every command. I realized as I sat there, that the idiot was in love with her. He'd done all of this because he loved her.

She dove into her purse, and pulled out a tiny packet of white powder, and his eyes lit up. "I didn't forget, you. Here, just as I promised."

He smiled as he took it. "You're amazing, Natalia." Then he looked me in the eye and said, "The boy wasn't supposed to get hurt. I'd never hurt a kid."

"You *did* hurt a kid, dumbass."

Natalia opened her door and slid out, pulling me with her. Then she wrestled me into the driver's door of the "new" car, a sad looking Toyota, and kept her gun on me as I climbed over the console into the passenger seat.

Hank turned the pickup around while we got in and buckled up, and then Natalia twisted the key, and it started right up. She gave Hank a wave, and he went back the way we'd come from. Natalia backed the Toyota out and took off in the opposite direction. There didn't seem to be a soul around to notice the car being stolen. No one to report it. Mason wouldn't know what vehicle to search for.

Then Natalia pulled out my cell phone, and smiling evilly at me, said, "thumbprint, or I'll shoot you now instead of later."

I pressed my thumb to the phone so she could use it.

She tapped the microphone and said, "Jackson's Pond. Hurry." Then she tapped Send as tears filled my eyes.

"You're giving up Hank? Aren't you afraid he'll talk?"

"He's not going to talk. He's going to drive up to that lake, and then he's going to pull over and snort some of that cocaine. Only it's not cocaine. It's enough fentanyl powder to kill an elephant."

I gazed at her, horrified. "You're murdering him? But he loves you."

"Not as much as I love me." She dropped my phone back into her bag. I knew Mason was texting back. I knew he was, but I couldn't get to the phone.

"What are you going to do?" I asked. "Mason knows it's you. You shouldn't be wasting time with me, you should be running for the border by now."

She shrugged. "I have an exit strategy. I always have an exit strategy. Besides, I do have some compassion. When your detective lover finds Hank dead up there, he'll presume your body is somewhere in the lake. I wouldn't want him to be disappointed."

CHAPTER 10

I tried to walk through the patch of woods slowly, but Natalia DaVine kept poking me between the shoulder blades with her gun barrel. My footsteps crunched over twigs and debris, beneath gnarly river birch and willow trees, ever closer to the shore of a dark water pond.

"So you're just gonna shoot me?" I asked. I knew that was what she was planning. What I didn't know was why I was so calm about it. "You can seriously do that to me?"

"Why should it be harder to shoot you than anyone else?" I'd slowed a little. She poked me with the gun barrel. "Then you've done it before?" I asked.

"You ask too many questions."

"I don't see how you can refuse to answer the last questions of a woman about to die. How heartless are you, anyway?"

She sniffed hard, like her nose was stuffy, but kept walking. About ten steps later, she said, "No, I've never had to do anything like this before."

Okay, good, that's a point in our favor. Inner Bitch was decidedly more optimistic than I was. *Maybe she won't be able to go through with it. Give her reasons to doubt. Come on, talk. It's what you do best.*

Writing is what I do best, Inner Bitch.

Then write. Just do it out loud.

I took a breath. The pond was closer. I could see it. Only a few acres in size, but most of it was inaccessible due to the thick forest around it. It was lined with cat tails and reeds, and probably full of snapping turtles and bull-head. "I think killing me is gonna feel like killing a sister," I said.

"I fail to see why."

"We're both women. We're both authors in the same field. We're both psychics."

We're not fucking psychic, Inner Bitch said. It was a kneejerk reaction to the word, one we usually shared.

If it helps us survive this, we are.

"That's new," Natalia said. "A few minutes ago, you were calling me a phony, a fraud, a liar—"

"I have a temper. It's my biggest flaw. So shoot me." I bit my lip. "Not really."

She actually laughed. Just a little, but still.

"I've been thinking about it, though, and it hit me that

you must have something. That exercise you gave me worked like a charm."

Natalia nodded. "Of course it did."

"And there's the fact that I can't read you. You're like a brick wall." The only other person I had this much trouble reading was Mason. But it turned out I didn't need to read him because we were just two halves of the same whole.

"I block when I'm around another gifted individual."

Gifted individual. Now there was an interesting term for it. "You can block? I didn't know that was possible." I stopped walking and turned to face her. It was an impulse move, not preplanned. I was genuinely into the conversation, I guess. It was much more fun than my impending demise.

She stopped walking too and stood there, holding her gun pointed at my chest, her eyes never quite meeting mine. The wind smelled like seaweed and lake water. It smelled like home.

"I'd love to learn how to do that," I said softly.

"I assumed you already knew. I haven't been able to read you either."

I frowned. "Maybe...gifted people can't read each other?"

She shook her head. "I've read others. Maybe you do it automatically. A reflex."

I nodded. "I can never read Mason very well, either. I've always thought his cop-sense was a lot like my NFP."

"NFP?"

I smiled a little. "For not fucking psychic. It's kind of an inside joke between Mason and the boys and me." A wave of pain rose up in my gut and tears burned my eyes. "Those poor kids. They lost their father, then their mother went batshit and had to be locked up in a max security psych facility. I don't know if they can handle losing me, too."

She blinked a few times. I was getting to her, maybe. "I wish there was another way, Rachel, but it's you or me."

"Killing me isn't going do any good. Mason knows it was you. By now so does the entire department."

"I don't need anything but time." She waggled her gun. "And you're wasting it. Turn around and get moving."

I didn't obey, just tried to get her to meet my eyes. "We're in the middle of nowhere. It would take me an hour, maybe two, to hike to a phone from here. Take the car and go. You can be a hundred miles away before I make it that far."

"Turn around and move!"

Her voice had gone cold. So I turned and moved. But I kept on talking. "If your gift is for real, then why did you have to resort to fake kidnappings? Why couldn't you help with real ones?"

"Use my powers for good, you mean?" Her tone dripped sarcasm. She nudged me with her gun.

I took another step and water rose up around my feet. The ground was squishy nearer the shore. The air smelled fishy and wet. There was a reedy border of cattails and mush. Mud oozed into my shoes, and it clung and sucked at my feet as I tried to keep walking.

"I did for a while, you know," she said. "Used my gift to help people. After that first little boy I helped to save, I was a hero. People adored me. There were thousands of letters and emails, begging for my help. And I tried, I did. But it was hit and miss. You know how it is, you get bits and pieces, and it's anybody's guess what they mean."

"I do know. It's only in hindsight you can fit it all together sometimes."

"And by then it's too late," she whispered.

I stood stock still, water and mud slowly creeping up around the tops of my shoes. "One of them died, didn't they? One of the kids you tried to help?"

She didn't answer but she didn't nudge me to get moving again either, so I turned to look at her over my shoulder. Her entire body was trembling, and her eyes were filling. She wasn't focused on me so much as looking at something inside her own mind, I thought, so I turned all the way around to face her.

"That's it, isn't it? You hired on to help solve an abduction and couldn't find the victim."

"I found him," she said. "I got the images. I pieced it together. I led the police right to him." Her lips pulled tight, a grotesque grimace. "But he was already...." She closed her eyes, squeezed them really tight.

As sorry as I felt for her in that moment, I also saw my

chance. I swung my clasped fists down as hard as I could on her gun hand. The weapon fell, dropping right into the mud and sinking out of sight. Her eyes flew open, filled with rage, and she lunged at me, grabbing for my throat. I tried to take a step back, but the mud sucked at my shoes, and we both went over, me on my back and her on top of me. The wet muck rose up around my body, and I struggled to keep my head up. Her weight and her hands around my neck pushed me deeper. The mud was cold and thick on my ears, my cheeks, my chin.

I strained to keep my face from being submerged. She was strangling me and pushing my head down. Dammit, I was younger and I was stronger, I should be able to take her, but she had the advantage. I tried to use my hands to push myself up, but I was pushing against liquid. Nothing solid. The mud closed over my eyes, my nose. I twisted and writhed, my hands clawing for a hold.

And then I felt the gun.

I closed my hand around it, finding the grips, getting hold of the weapon, sliding my finger around the trigger, tipping the nose up and praying it wouldn't backfire and blow my hand off.

I didn't have a choice. I had to take a breath or pass out and drown as mud filled my lungs. I squeezed the trigger, felt the weapon buck in my hand and heard its muffled boom.

And suddenly the hands around my neck fell away. I tipped my head forward, raising my face from the mud and gasping, blinking my eyes clear. I swiped mud off my face with my free hand. Her weight was still on my body, but I managed to get an arm between us, and I shoved her one way while wriggling myself the other, and eventually managed to get her off me. Finally, I sat up, fighting the muck to do it.

She lay still, facedown beside me. I got up to my feet, shoved the muddy gun into my jeans, and bent to roll Natalia over and tug her into shallower gunk.

She sucked in a ragged breath as mud slid down the sides of her face. Her eyes opened, and she gazed up at me, unfocused, confused. "You shot me."

"I know. I'm sorry."

She took a breath. "It was easier finding kids I knew for sure would be okay."

"Those kids would have been okay to begin with," I said. "They didn't need your help. You traumatized them for nothing."

"I couldn't face...finding another body."

"Then you should've found a different line of work, Natalia. This bullshit we have...it means something. It's *for* something." For the first time, I really believed that. This stuff of mine, my NFP, it could be hellish. It could be a burden, a heavy one, and sometimes, a nightmare.

But there was purpose behind it. A purpose that had nothing to do with fame or wealth. Natalia was a living example of what happened when you turned your back on that purpose.

I held out a hand. "Come on, get up out of the mud."

"I don't think there's any point," she said.

I noticed then, the red tinted mud that covered her chest. It was growing redder. "We have to try. Come on."

She shook her head, closed her eyes. And then she changed. I can't describe it visually. There was just an instant when she changed from a person, to a body. From a living being to an empty husk. It's unmistakable when it happens, yet it's invisible.

She was gone. She'd vacated her body, and the mud no longer mattered. There was no way I could move her onto dry land, so I slogged my way back up onto the shore, and jogged back to the stolen car, mud dripping off me all the way. I opened the door and rummaged in Natalia's bag for her phone. And then I quickly called Mason.

He answered on the first ring, and choked out my name in a voice so hoarse with emotion I almost didn't recognize it.

"It's me, Mace. I'm okay."

"Thank God. Where are you, babe?"

"On the other side of the lake from where she sent Hank. Is he—"

"We found him unconscious. He's on his way to the ER by chopper."

"Tell 'em it was fentanyl powder. He snorted it."

"Where is Natalia?" he asked.

I closed my eyes. "Dead. I...shot her."

"Hell."

"I didn't have a choice."

"You didn't have to tell me that. I know. I'm on my way."

I nodded. "Don't hang up, okay?" My throat was tight, the emotion of the whole thing suddenly hitting me like a ton of that lake mud.

"I'm not hanging up."

I was shivering, both with cold and probably some kind of shock. I touched the phone's speaker button and got into the stolen car, mud and all. The keys were still in the switch, so I started it up, closed the door, cranked on the heat.

"Are you sure you're okay?" Mason asked.

"I think so. I'm soaked and muddy and cold."

"I see you," he said.

There was no way he'd made the trip that fast, I thought. And then I heard the helicopter, and within a few seconds it was touching down and Mason was climbing out and running toward me. I got out of the car, but my shivering was so violent I felt like it would pull my muscles right off my bones.

Then he was there, wrapping me up in the blanket he carried, and in his arms. He held me against him, and his warmth seeped into me, and I just went limp. It was okay now. It was truly okay.

He scooped me right up and carried me back to the helicopter.

"But Natalia. She's out there, in the mud—" I heard

sirens in the distance, knew the cavalry was only seconds away. They would handle everything. Mason climbed into the helicopter with me, holding me on his lap, those strong arms never easing their firm embrace.

"Let's get her to the hospital," he told the pilot.

"I don't need—"

"Yeah you do. Just relax now, let me take care of you, okay?"

There was no point fighting it. I was too cold and still shaking too hard to fight it. As the helicopter carried me toward what I hoped would be a very warm ER, I thought about Natalia, and me, and the "gift" we shared.

"She wasn't a fake," I said. "She really did have...you know. *It*. But she found a kid's body early on, and I think it...I think it broke her, somehow."

"Doesn't justify kidnapping or attempted murder, Rache."

"I know." I relaxed my head against his chest. "But I get it. I get how this...this stuff could be...too much."

Mason's hand stroked my hair off my forehead. "Even for you?"

I opened my eyes and looked at his worried ones. Only days ago, I'd been afraid my NFP had deserted me, and I'd been frantically trying to find a way to get it back. And now, I wondered if that had been a mistake. Or if it was even up to me.

"Rachel? Do you feel like it could break you, too?"

"I hope not," I whispered. "But the truth is, I think getting broken is probably an occupational hazard."

He pressed his palm to my cheek. "Not for you, babe. Not for you. You have backup. You have a family behind you. Jeremy, Josh, Myrtle, Hugo."

"My Scooby gang," I said. I was starting to feel warm again.

"And me," he said. "You've got me. I'm your safety net. I'll never let you fall, Rachel. I promise. Never."

"I'm counting on it." A little more of the chill faded. His warmth chased it away. "I love you, Mason."

"Love you back, Rache. And I've got you." He hugged me a little tighter. "I've got you."

THE END

Continue reading for an excerpt from
***Girl Blue*, the next book in the Brown & DeLuca Series.**

PREVIEW GIRL BLUE

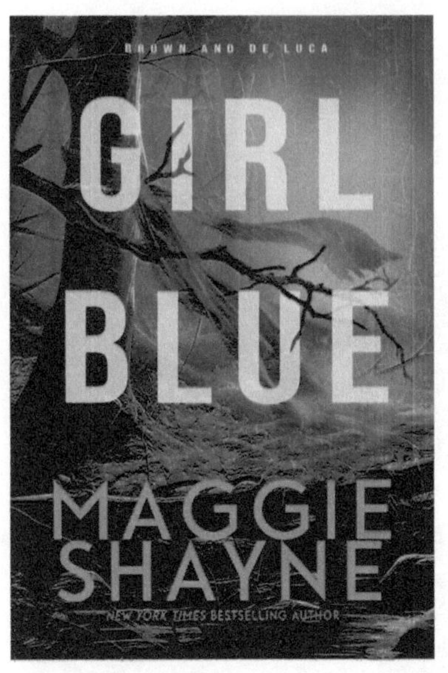

CHAPTER 1

I was waiting, crouched behind his car in the parking lot. It was dark, and there were street lights but no cameras. I'd checked ahead of time. I'd planned this carefully, because I was going to kill him, no matter what. I figured I'd make it as easy as possible.

He came out of the bar, three sheets to the wind, which would make things so much easier. He listed to one side but tried real hard to stand up straight as he walked around the parking lot, awash in android-blue light, looking for his car. Then he took his key fob out and tapped it. The car beside me unlocked its doors and flashed its headlights. He saw it and smiled like he'd just won the lottery.

Only he hadn't won anything. His winning days were over.

He staggered to the car, opened the driver's door. I

slipped up behind him, silent as a shadow, and jabbed him in the crease of his ass with a perfectly placed needle.

He spun around like a wobbling top, about to fall over. "What the hell!" he said and clocked me in the jaw. My head snapped sideways. I'd have gone down if I hadn't caught myself on the roof of his car. I stood ready to take another blow, thinking it would've been worse if he wasn't so drunk and wondering how long the drug would take to kick in.

He had one hand on his ass where I'd stuck him. His eyes rolled. I grabbed his shirt front, pulled him toward me as I opened the back door of his car. Then I turned him around, because I could not do this looking at him, and shoved him face-first onto the back seat. I climbed in after him, right up his back. He was out cold in seconds, not moving. I took the wood-handled garrote from my pocket. I'd made it out of picture-frame wire, several layers twisted together to make it thick, so I wouldn't acciden-tally decapitate him. I gagged a little as I put it over his head, and pulled it down between his face and the seat, over his chin to his neck. My inner voice, though it wasn't *really* mine, said, *Do it. Just do it. There's no other way. He won't feel anything. Just do it. You're so close.*

I pulled the right handle with my left hand, the left handle with my right, so they crossed at his nape. It was awful, what I was doing. My lips pulled back from my teeth with the effort it took—and not just physically. I had to *force* myself and my *self* was resisting. Tears filled my eyes. I tried to focus on my watch. It was an old-school watch, not a smart one. A delicate oval, with gold numbers and hands that swept way too slowly around its face. A narrow, pink leather band. After two minutes, he started to convulse, his body bucking underneath me, just like the internet said he would. I pulled tighter, to hold on, pressing my knees into his back like a cowboy at a rodeo. Terrible sounds started coming from him. Wet, growly, choky sounds. I wiped my wet face against my black, spandex-covered shoulder.

Just hold on. It's almost over. It's better this way. For every-one, even him.

I didn't know how many times the second hand had circled, but eventually it felt like it was over. The sounds stopped first, thank God. I'd never get them out of my head, though. Those sounds would haunt my dreams for the rest of my life. In silence, the twitching of his body eased, and he finally went still. I looked at my wristwatch and held the wood and wire weapon as tight as I could for three more minutes. My arm muscles were cramping up. My hands hurt despite the thick leather gloves I wore to protect them. Murder was not easy.

When I was sure he was dead, I let go of the garrote, slid it out from beneath him, and then climbed off him and backed down his body and out of the car. My legs were shaking so hard I wasn't sure I could stand up. But I did, I stood there beside the open car door, looking in at the man on the back seat.

I sniffed, backhanded my nose with my black leather glove, forced my gaze away from him to look around. A dozen vehicles, but no people. No witnesses. His keys were on the pavement, so I picked them up. His legs were still sticking out of the car. I bent them at the knees, so I could close the door.

Then I got behind the wheel and started the car, noticing for the first time that it was a Jaguar, a newish one. Blue or black, impossible to tell which in the dark.

I knew exactly where to put him. There was a burlap bag and a shovel already there, waiting.

I started the car. The radio blasted to life, scaring me so bad my head hit the ceiling before I got hold of myself and snapped the thing off. Then I sat there, gripping the wheel, white-knuckled. I took three long, deep breaths. Okay. I was okay. I put the car into gear and pulled out of the parking lot and onto the road.

I was driving through the night with a dead guy in the back seat, shaking all the way to my marrow. This was not me. This was not anything I'd ever imagined myself capable of, not in my wildest dreams.

Well, maybe in my *wildest* dreams.

A congested moan came from the back seat and sent a lightning bolt through my entire being.

The alarm clock went off like a freaking mind bomb.

The murderous dream popped like a balloon at a birthday party, showering its deadly latex bits all around me. I sat up fast, blurting an overly loud, "Holy fuck!"

Mason sprang out of bed, landing in a ready crouch beside it. "What? What?"

My bulldog picked up her head, blinked sightlessly at me, then lowered it and resumed snoring.

I looked around our bedroom like I was searching for an explanation. But there were only the soothing green walls and rich walnut trim.

"Rachel?" Mason turned on the lamp.

I couldn't look at him. Not yet. Lingering sparks of murder were still blinking out one by one in my head. I swallowed hard. "I'm okay. Bad dream."

"Was it?"

I met his eyes. "You know me too well."

"So? What was it?"

"I don't know yet."

Yes, you do. It's not like it's the first time a killer took up residence in your head, or you took up residence in his, after all.

It's not that, Inner Bitch.

Then what is it?

Like I just told Mason, I don't know yet.

Yes, you do.

"You okay?"

I slid up out of our big bed, planted a big, morning-breathy kiss on his face, and said, "I'd be better with coffee."

He smacked my butt and said, "Then coffee you shall have." He pulled on a pair of pajama bottoms and a T-shirt that said, DEFINITELY NOT A COP. Yes, I bought it for him. I think it's hilarious. He only wears it to humor me. What can I say? I've got myself a keeper.

I turned back toward the bed. "Wanna go outside, Myrt?"

Myrtle did not so much as twitch her ears in reply. "I guess not." I pulled on my fluffiest robe because it was six a.m. and also September, and went out onto the balcony. It had pretty wrought iron railings and a view of the four-mile-long, mile-wide Whitney Point Reservoir.

God, I loved *seeing*. I could spend hours just...seeing. As would, I guessed, anyone who'd spent twenty years of their life blind. I went to the railing and looked at the water. It was a rippled mirror, reflecting rolling hills and blue sky. The air tasted good, but its flavor was shifting. It smelled like back-to-school.

When Mason returned, he not only had our coffees, but a pair of blankets over his arm. He set the steaming mugs on the railing, and spread the blankets over our bowl-shaped wicker chairs in case there was dew on the cushions. I sank into mine, pulled the blanket around me, and he handed me my mug.

"You are the perfect man," I said. "I don't know if you know it or not, but–"

"I do know it." He dropped the second blanket on his chair, but didn't sit. He stood by the railing like I'd been doing. Only he wasn't looking, like I had been. He was thinking.

My man was a bit of a thinker. It was his greatest flaw.

"You miss Jeremy." It wasn't a question.

He glanced back at me. "I just don't *get* living on campus when campus is only thirty minutes away."

Three weeks ago, we'd moved Jeremy into his Binghamton University dorm. Mason seemed to think we'd moved him to the moon. "It's Labor Day weekend, Mace. He'll probably be back before breakfast and not leave again until Tuesday morning."

"Yeah." He still sounded mopey. "Think we'll see him this time, or he'll just drop off his laundry and go hang with his friends?"

"Wow. Clingy much?"

"Misty sees more of him than we do."

"You're an uncle. Misty is a girl, and she's better look-ing. Plus, she has her aunt's DNA, so I don't know how you can blame him. You know the females of the de Luca line are irresistible."

He sighed, staring out at the water. I stretched my leg to kick his backside. "That was funny. You didn't even crack a smile."

"Sorry. You're right. I know."

"Kids grow up. It happens. Get over it."

"Right. You were the one sniffling all the way home the day we moved him in."

"Freaking campus is a pollen pit. Sue me."

"You don't have allergies."

"Did that day."

I slid over in my chair, opened my blanket and patted the spot beside me. "BU is lots closer than the police academy, you know. You'd better toughen up by the time Jere heads to Albany." I was talking a good game, but I was missing Jeremy as much as Mason was. We might only be an uncle and an honorary aunt, but we'd been raising the boys for two years, and they felt like our own kids. Even though I wasn't nearly old enough for that.

Mason started to get in with me, then stopped because there was a ping from his PJ pocket. He pulled out his phone and looked at it.

"I reiterate my opinion," I said, "that this balcony should be a device-free zone."

"No such thing for a cop." He tapped the screen and said, "What's up, Rosie?"

Rosie was his partner. I hoped he was calling to invite us over for a barbecue.

At six-something a.m?

Yeah, probably not, I thought in reply to Inner Bitch's query. *I just hope it's not about what I dreamed.*

But it is. You know that, right?

I kind of did, but I didn't want to admit it. Not even to

my subconscious Chatty Cathy.

Mason put the phone back into his pocket, and I'd missed whatever else he'd said. But his face looked more serious than before. "I've gotta go. We have a body."

I closed my eyes. "A body?"

"Yeah. Joggers found him off the Rail Trial."

I could see the man from my dream in my mind's eye. A youthful fifty-something, fit, clean shaven, hair so light it was hard to spot the gray unless you were up close to it, with a yellow-orange tint like it had been red once. He had a perfectly bald spot the size of a silver dollar on the back of his head. I'd stared at that spot for an eternity last night.

A forefinger hooked under my chin. I opened my eyes to see my guy's worried ones trying to get a peek inside my head. He said, "Anything you need to tell me, Rachel?"

"Only if he drove a dark-colored Jag and was strangled. Or mostly strangled."

"Mostly strangled?"

"I woke up before he was all the way strangled. Might've had to bash his head in with a rock or something to get the job done, for all I know."

He swore softly, sinking onto the edge of my bowl chair, no easy feat. "You okay?"

"It was pretty vivid. He spun around and punched me in the jaw, and I swear it actually aches this morning." I tested my mouth-hinges experimentally, and sure as shit, the right one felt tender. "Then I was kneeling on his back, choking the life out of him with some kind of homemade garrote."

"Do you want to come along?" he asked.

"I don't want to leave Josh home alone."

"He's thirteen."

"Yeah, but I don't know what this is yet. So—"

"You saying it feels dangerous to you?"

"It feels...personal. Close." I rubbed my arms, set down my coffee and used his shoulders to pull myself up out of my comfy nest. "I need to shower. Like, now."

"So do I. Let me call in."

I went in to start without him.

The clay-tiled shower was double sized, with multiple heads. I adjusted the water, stepped in and let the hot spray blast the remnants of that dream away. There wasn't *always* a killer dragging me into mental ride-alongs, but it had been known to happen. The first time, it had been Mason's dead, serial-killer brother. Long story, but suffice it to say I got a little something extra from Eric Conroy Brown along with his donated corneal tissue. He opened some kind of door.

I knew things, felt things. I called it NFP for Not Fucking Psychic because I don't believe in psychics.

Mason stepped into the tiled shower. He moved into the spray beside me, turned around and scrubbed his hair. I watched him until he opened his eyes and looked back at me. And then he pushed my wet hair off my face, and tucked it behind my ear, and gave me that look that said everything I needed to hear. And I forgot what I'd been so upset about.

Mason was worried about Rachel. She'd been shaken by her dream. It had taken minutes for the fear to leave her eyes.

He parked where there was room, got out of his restored (by him) '74 Monte Carlo, and headed down Binghamton's popular walking trail. It ran alongside the Susquehanna River. Pleasant, usually. Not so much, now. Uniforms, forensics people, and his partner Rosie stood around a pile of freshly turned black earth, and a burlap shroud that wasn't quite big enough. A pale, dead arm stuck out from elbow to fingertips. Looked like the corpse was waving hello.

He walked closer. The murmur of the river drowned out the sounds of singing birds. The body was in a hole, sort of.

"Not even deep enough to cover the poor SOB," Rosie said. He had lost twenty pounds on his latest diet, which showed exactly nowhere. He was a big guy, his Rosie. They'd been partners since their rookie days. "Jogger spotted his hand, just sticking up outta the dirt. Can you imagine?"

"It'll make a great story, I guess."

"Yeah, eventually."

"Why the burlap? Why not just bury him?" Mason walked around the shallow grave to the bag's opening, picked up an edge with a pencil, and peered inside. "Flashlight?" he asked, hand out. Someone gave him one, cold steel cylinder in his palm, and he aimed it. "Ligature marks. Looks like he was strangled." *Or mostly strangled.* Something tickled up his spine. He shrugged it away.

"Anyone find an ID on him?" he asked.

"We're not patting him down for a wallet until we get him home where we can do it right." That was spoken with authority from a redhead with an ultra-short haircut. "Bag him up, burlap and all," she ordered. "Move him as little as possible. Don't shake off trace evidence."

As the team scrambled, she grinned at Mason. It was probably disrespectful to think she looked just like a Christmas elf. She had dimples, pink cheeks, intelligent green eyes, and a hairline that made her ears look ever so slightly pointed.

And she had her hand out, he finally noticed.

"Billie Carmichael. I'm the new forensic pathologist."

Thinking she looked about fourteen probably proved that he was getting old. "Mason Brown," he said.

"I know who you are, Detective Brown. I know your wife, too. I'm a huge fan."

"She's not my—"

"Careful!" The techs had dropped the body onto the gurney a little too hard, and the burlap came open.

Mason glimpsed the guy's face, either pudgy or

starting to swell. His hair was mostly a pale orangey-gray. He looked back at the redhead. "What's an FP doing at a crime scene?"

"It's my first case. I couldn't wait." She said it with a grin, then forced a more serious expression.

"Since he's already bagged, you want to give me the rundown?" he asked. He was trying to remember ever being that happy to be at work, and failing.

"Male, mid-fifties, maybe a drinker. He was probably dumped last night," Billie Carmichael said. He liked her confident tone. "There's a car back by the trail head. Nobody else around. Might be his."

Rosie met Mason's eyes, brows raised, clearly impressed.

"What kind of car?" Mason asked.

"Jag," the new FP replied. "Nice one. Man I'd hate to die and leave a ride like that behind."

"Shit," Mason shook his head. "Shit."

His phone buzzed. It would be Rachel, asking about all this. He wished he didn't have to tell her, but knew he did. They didn't keep stuff from each other.

He walked a little bit away before looking at the text.

"Don't forget, BBQ at noon. Wayward nephew and all."

He got a good feeling from that message. He looked at Billie, and said, "You gonna be a while with the unboxing?"

"The unboxing. That's funny." Mason didn't smile,

and she turned all business again. "I'm gonna work straight through the day on this guy."

"Good. I need to go home after I finish up here. Will you call me when I can come and get a look at the victim?"

"Yeah, sure."

Rosie said, "The Jag in the parking area is registered to Dwayne Clark. Got an address, phone number, and email. We're getting more info now."

"You got a phone number, you said?"

Rosie nodded, showing Mason his iPad.

"That's a cell number." Mason tapped it into the keypad of his phone, then silenced it and listened.

The guy in the burlap bag started ringing.

"Guess we've got a probable ID." He ended the call. "Let's get some background on him."

"Already under way," Rosie said.

"Okay, good." He looked at the ground around the makeshift grave. There were plenty of tracks in the dirt, thanks to the team that had dug the body out. "I hope you got a lot of shots of the ground before it was trampled," he said to the cop with the camera.

"I did." He brought his camera over and scrolled photos across its digital screen.

Mason looked at the images of the undisturbed grave. The killer had barely dug past the grass's knotted root carpet. He'd chopped it open, rolled it back, scraped out a little of the dirt underneath, and then tried to cover the unfortunate Dwayne Clark with it again.

Mason said, "Whoever put him here expected him to be found. Anything the body and this scene have to tell us could be significant. Let's not miss anything."

Billie's guys carried the dead man to an ambulance that had driven over the grass to get close. "The forensics team will finish up here," she said. "I want to stay with the body."

Mason said. "Listen, Carmichael, just so you know, we sometimes use Rachel as a consultant on cases like this."

"I know." Her elf-green eyes popped wider. "Are you bringing her in on *this one*? Wow, I didn't think I'd get to work with her so soon."

Oh, hell. "Listen, if you fangirl all over Rachel, she'll make you her slave. If you want her respect, treat her like an equal." It was a dumb request. Rachel had no equal, but still.

The change in Billie's expression was so sudden and deliberate he almost laughed. "I'll be completely professional, Detective. And I'll call you when I've finished the autopsy." Then she unlocked her phone and handed it to him.

He entered his number into her contacts, then returned the phone. "Thanks."

As he walked back to his car, Mason made a mental to-do list. He had to go home, host a family barbecue, and during a free moment break it to Rachel that her link to the darkness was back, big time.

CHAPTER 2

Jeremy had arrived home before nine, stuffed the washer with more laundry than it could possibly clean, helped himself to 80% of what was in the fridge, and answered my, "how was your week?" while he ate it.

I stood across the counter from him, trying to interpret his food-muffled words. "Are you too short on time to chew and swallow before talking? Gonna eat the last crumb and then launch yourself out of here at the speed of teen?"

He stopped talking, finished chewing, took a big gulp of milk. "Sorry, Rache."

"*Aunt* Rache."

He grinned. "I *am* in a hurry, though."

Josh, sitting opposite his big brother, sighed with all

the drama thirteen can muster–which is, I have discovered, a *lot*. He slid off the stool and headed for the door. Hugo, Myrtle's sighted, male mini-me, was on his heels. There is nothing in the entire universe cuter than an English bulldog puppy. Hugo had also become Myrtle's seeing-eye pal.

Myrt remained where she was, sitting on the floor by Jeremy, who had dropped enough crumbs to make it worth her while.

Josh slammed the door hard enough to make me wince.

Should've made the place kid proof, Inner bitch opined.

There's no such thing, I thought in reply.

"What's with him, Rache?" Jeremy asked.

I sent him my patented glare, which I had learned from my sister, who had learned it from our mother, may she rest in peace.

"*Aunt* Rache," he corrected. "Jeeze, what's everybody so touchy about, anyway?"

"You're neglecting your brother, not to mention your dogs and your uncle. These are dire offenses, Jeremy Brown. Just because you're a big college man now doesn't mean you get to blow off your family."

"I've barely been gone three weeks!"

"Yeah, and you're already acting like a big fat douchebag. Spend the morning with your brother."

"You can't tell me what to do anymore. I'm an adult."

I shrugged. "An adult wouldn't act the way you're acting."

"And how am I acting?"

"Like a selfish little shithead."

That pissed him off. I was kind of pissed too, but since I was technically the grownup in the room, I notched myself down a few degrees. "We're having a barbecue here at noon. My sister and Jim and the twins will be here. You and Misty can take off after, and you've got the rest of the long weekend to be together. I'm gonna come crash in your dorm room if you don't spend some time with the fam. Mason's moping like Myrtle when her dish is empty. Josh is heartbroken, and don't even get me started on the dogs."

Myrtle chose that moment to whap him in the shin with her paw. He'd stopped dropping crumbs and she didn't like it.

He looked down at the dog, then out the window at Josh. His kid bro was walking slow with his head down. Hugo was trotting beside him with a frisbee in his mouth, but Josh didn't even notice.

Jeremy said, "I'm sorry. I had a hard week."

"You wanna talk about it?"

"I've got this one professor who's a Class-A asshat."

"Language. You want me to come down there and kick him in the balls?"

The trouble in his eyes evaporated. He even smiled a

little. "Yes, Aunt Rachel, I want you to come down there and kick him in the balls."

He slid off the stool, smacked his thighs and said, "Wanna go hunt some froggies, Myrtle? Froggies? Hmm?"

Myrt sprang upright and started wiggling her butt.

"I'd like to hear more about the asshat professor, though," I said.

"Later. And...I'll do better. With the family."

His mea culpa look was so much like Mason's that my heart melted.

"I know you will. We miss the hell out of you, you know."

"You, too?"

"Me especially," I admitted. "I love you, kid."

"I love you, too."

"Well, duh."

Mason grilled steaks, looking like the most content man on the planet for the first time in three weeks. My sister Sandra had brought mac salad and coleslaw. I heated up a can of baked beans in the microwave, poured chips into giant bowls and scooped dip into small ones.

Yeah, I don't cook. It's not what I was put on the planet to do.

"Let's eat down by the water," Sandra said. We had just exited the house, our arms full of plates and silverware. "Pretty soon it'll be too cold."

"I concur." And then I whistled to get the kids' attention. "Will you guys move the picnic tables down by the water for us?"

Jeremy and my niece Misty, who'd been sitting side by side on the dock holding hands, got up and came running. Josh, too, dogs flanking him. Christie stayed put and returned her attention to her phone. Misty and Christie were twins, blue-eyed blondes like their mother, although you'd never know it today, as Christie wore a crocheted hat, with bright colored concentric circles, and it covered every lock. Jim, world's greatest brother-in-law, left his position as official grilling commentator to help them lug the old-fashioned wooden picnic table.

"Jeremy got over being mad at you?" Sandra asked.

"He couldn't deny his own assholery."

"Is that a real word?"

"It is now. As an author, I get to add new words to the language."

"I don't think that's true."

"I'm pretty sure it is. Sprounce is one of mine. You know, what Myrt does when she finds a froggie. Sprounce." I made claw hands under the plates and bounced a little.

"I love you," she said.

"Me, too."

We walked across the dirt drive that wasn't really a road, because we were the only ones who used it, to the picnic table on the grassy patch of shoreline. The kids had already taken off, but Jere was still within earshot. I said, "I appreciate you hanging out with us today. I won't be upset if you two want to go do your own thing after we eat." I was careful not to sound like I was giving permission in front of everyone. I knew how I would react to that—instantly and with great fury—and presumed he'd be the same.

"We'll probably hang out for a while," he said. "Maybe take off later, though."

Sandra and I put the plates on the table, and I glanced over at Christie. Her full attention was on her device. I pulled out my phone and texted her, "Get off your fucking phone."

She looked up from the screen, grinning at me. "You are so ridiculous, Aunt Rache," she said, getting up, pocketing it, and walking in that way only super tall, super lean teenage girls can do. Then she pulled off her hat to release a cascade of dead-straight, jet-black hair.

I bit back the sound of horror that jumped into my mouth. Well, mostly bit it back. Half a squeak escaped. Sandra elbowed me in the small of my back, where her kid couldn't see. When I could speak, I said, "Wow, what an... extreme change."

The guys were carrying the steaks to the table, and everyone was finding a spot to sit.

"I got sick of people not being able to tell us apart."

"So you decided to become the evil twin?"

"*Rachel*!" Sandra scolded.

"She knows I'm teasing. You know I'm teasing, right?" I took a plate and a seat on the bench. Mason slid in beside me.

"I know you're teasing," Christie said. "Besides, I already *was* the evil twin. At least now I look the part."

"I've seen evil, kid," Mason said. "You ain't it."

"But it's nice to have goals," I added in my best Sandra tones.

That made her smile. Christie wasn't such a puzzle to me. She kind of *was* me. Ninety-nine percent attitude and convinced of her rightness on all subjects, regardless of evidence to the contrary.

She wasn't evil. If she were suddenly orphaned and I left the planet, she could probably go either way, but as things stood, she was going to be okay.

I looked her over thoroughly, nodding slow. "You should darken your brows a little bit."

"I hate makeup."

"Not makeup. Dye. I'll have Amy text you her brand. You now, she's naturally a redhead, right?"

"No way!"

"Way. Not since she's been my goth-Friday, but I was at her mother's place once, and there are pictures. Total ginger." A platter of food came my way before we could discuss my assistant any further. Amy does a million jobs. Most importantly, she posts as me on social media because I have zero tolerance for idiots. If I were Tweeting every day, my career would go up in smoke, you know, unless I were president.

I stabbed a big juicy steak, dropped it onto my plate, and enjoyed the friendly chaos of conversation going on around me. We talked so much when were together I didn't know how anyone ate. But we managed to decimate the meal, and get through dessert–apple pie with ice cream. It grew eerily silent once we had *that* in front of us.

We really were a family. Not officially or anything, but I was starting to wonder if Mason was ever going to ask.

Right. And it's what year, now?

I know, Inner Bitch, I know...but if I ask, he might say no.

He won't.

He could.

He won't.

Myrtle growled, which Myrtle almost never did. Hugo immediately jumped in front of her and started snarfing. (Snarf: Snuffly barking, which is what bulldogs do. Yes, it's another of my words, and also the only perfect word to describe this sound.) We looked where Hugo was looking, at a tall, young man with terrible posture, walking up our seldom used dirt road toward us.

I got to my feet, still nervous from last night's murder dream. Mason got up, too, stepped over the picnic bench and headed toward the guy. The stranger lifted a hand. He was looking right at me and smiling. "Rachel? Wow, it's really you!"

Oh my God, a fan, Inner Bitch said.

Fans put these steaks on the table, IB.

Yeah, but they don't get to show up at our house.

I kind of agreed with her on that one. The thing about writing airy-fairy self-help books like mine was that you occasionally attracted a batshit fan. Apparently, straight to your front door.

I went to stand beside Mason. Jeremy was on his feet, too, and so was the dark twin, with a distinctive touch-my-aunt-and-you-die glint shining from within her eyeliner. *She hates makeup, my ass,* Inner Bitch noted.

"It's really me," I said, polite, calm, not inviting or friendly. He had brown leaning-toward-gold eyes and thick lashes. His long brown hair hadn't seen shampoo in a while. He slouched like his backbone was tired. "What can I do for you?"

He was smiling really hard. "I just...there's so much. There's so much. I'm Gary. Conklin. I read everything of yours–" As he spoke, he came toward me, and Mason stepped right into his path.

He looked up at Mason. He was a head shorter. Had kind of a baby face. Round, with big eyes set deep that turned downward at the corners. "Whoa, man," he said, "You don't need to be worried about me." He leaned sideways, to see me around Mason. "I just...your books, it's like you're talking right to me."

"It feels like that to lots of readers," I said. "It means I'm doing something right."

"I have to talk to you, though. I walked all the way here."

I looked down at his feet. He was wearing sneakers that were more holes than canvas. "From where?"

"The shelter, um, St. Mary's."

"In Binghamton?" It was twenty miles south on 81.

He nodded.

"You want something to eat, Gary?"

"Rachel–" Mason turned fully, hands on my shoulders, leaning close, speaking soft. "This guy looks unstable," he said, for my ears only.

"Yeah, trust me I know. His head's a fucking cyclone. But his belly's empty."

"He could be dangerous."

"He reminds me of my brother."

The brother card got to him, but that's not why I played it. It was nothing but the truth.

"Gary, see the dock right there?" I asked, pointing at the square wooden dock that extended out from the shore. It was redwood stained with a railing all the way around and fish-pole holders mounted in four places. We had two Adirondack chairs out there, and a new one on the way, a double-wide one, for proper snuggling. "You go wait for me there. I'll bring you a plate of food and we'll talk a little, okay?"

"You don't have to feed me."

"We'll talk. Go, sit. Look at that peaceful lake. It's so calm. It always makes me feel better."

He looked at the water for a moment and I did, too. It was particularly placid today, its surface a smooth mirror reflecting the bright September sky. Finally, he gave a nod and went to the dock. He stood at the railing, despite the big chairs.

"I don't think this is a good idea, Rachel," Jim said. Jim, the quiet guy, who never rocked a single boat.

"I agree, but he's here and he's hungry. Besides, he's scrawny. Look at him, Jim. I could take him even if I was still blind. And you're right here, and Mason is coming over there with me, and I've got two strong kids here who'll kick his ass if he gets out of line. Not to mention Jeremy and Josh."

Misty smiled. Christie did not. She had the guy in her laser sites and wasn't even hearing me. My goodness, my niece was growing up kinda kick-ass. I liked it.

"Give me a few minutes." I was filling a plate as I spoke. We always cooked an extra steak to split up between the bulldogs, but they were going to have to muddle through with scraps this time.

"Keep the dogs here," I told Josh, who was my resident canine whisperer. Mason put an arm around my shoulders.

We hadn't had a chance to talk about the body that had been found this morning, because everyone had already arrived by the time he'd got back. And now certainly wasn't the time.

I said, "Hang back a little. I want him to feel safe."

"I want you to *be* safe."

"Perfect. Pick a distance that does both." I kissed his nose. "I love you." I said, in case the stranger was going to pull out a weapon and off me within the next few minutes. And I think Mason knew it.

The timing wasn't lost on me. This guy showing up the morning after a murder dream that might've been a...I don't want to say vision. It sounds so hokey. But yeah. That. Coincidence?

No such thing.

Sandra handed me silverware and a napkin, and I carried the food over to the dock. "Sit right here, Gary," I said, standing beside the chair. He came away from the railing, sat in the chair, and I handed him the food.

"Thank you. I haven't had anything today."

"I'll box you up some leftovers to take with you when you go. Go ahead, dig in. Get your belly full first, I can wait." And I wanted to wait. I wanted to feel him first, you know, with my NFP. I went to the railing myself, leaned my forearms on it, gazing out at the water while he ate. It was always easier to feel someone with my eyes closed, probably because I'd done it blind for so long, without even realizing I was doing it. It only became a full-blown thing though, after I got my new corneas. Mason thought, in hindsight, his brother must've had a touch of...what I had. But in Eric's case, it had made him crazy.

I closed my eyes and opened my radar. What I got felt like sparks from a live wire. I tried to focus harder, but it was just chaos.

Eventually the sounds of fork hitting plate went silent, and I turned to see that Gary had cleaned it. He leaned forward to set his empty dish on the decking.

"So first, you should know, I don't usually do this. Meet one-on-one with readers like this."

"Yeah, I–I know."

"What did you want to talk to me about?"

"Your books, they say things happen to you because you think about them."

I nodded slowly. "That's a very simplified explanation. You attract the *essence* of what you think about, believe in, and expect."

"Isn't that what I said?"

"Not exactly. Say you think about dogs all the time. That doesn't mean a dog's gonna show up. It all depends on how you feel about dogs when you're thinking about them. If you're afraid of dogs, and you think about dogs all the time, other things you're afraid of will start showing up. Could be a dog, could be a stalker."

Did you just say stalker? To a fan who walked here from Binghamton to meet you? Freudian slip much?

"You understand?" I asked, to drown out the rightness of Inner Bitch's comment.

"I don't have a problem with dogs. I like dogs."

A swing and a miss!

"What *do* you have a problem with, Gary?"

"Bad stuff." Storm clouds darkened his eyes.

"Bad stuff," I repeated, and I sent Mason a yellow alert sort of look. He was standing under a river birch six feet away. He could make it to me in two long strides. But the kid could probably stab me faster.

We should've searched him, Inner Bitch said.

Now you think of it. "What kind of bad stuff?"

Honest to God, I didn't feel any threat coming from him. Hatred and anger wafted off him, but it wasn't directed at me. I usually felt that sort of thing like prickles on my skin, only not on my skin, exactly.

Gary looked away, tipping his chin down just the way my brother Tommy used to do. There was something about him. I wanted to bring him inside and clean him up and fix his life.

Like you tried to do with Tommy.

Yeah, IB. Just like that.

"What kinds of bad things, Gary?"

And he flipped just like that, jumped out of the chair and glared at me, and then Mason was in between us, hands on the kid's shoulders, saying, "Okay, now. Everything's cool here, right? We're okay here, aren't we, Gary?"

I stayed behind Mason's body like the Cowardly Lion, thinking yep, he *could* get to me fast enough, after all. Gary's eyes had turned fiery, and he thrust out an arm, pointing at me. "You're wrong, Rachel de Luca! I *don't* think bad thoughts, but they come anyway. They come anyway and I can't make them stop!"

Mason's voice was much harsher when he said, "All right, Gary, it's time for you to go now. You crossed a line coming here, and it better not happen again. You understand me? It's not okay, coming here like this."

And just like that, the fire was doused. Puppy dog eyes blinked at me through the lingering smoke. "It's not okay I came here?"

"It would be better if you asked first. That's all," I said.

Are you out of your fucking mind?

Mason's eyes asked me the very same question.

"I'd rather be blind than to feel the way you do right now," I told Gary. "I'm really sorry you're going through this." I meant it.

He relaxed, like a full-body sigh. "Do you know what it is, Rachel? What's making the bad thoughts come?"

"I know people who would. People who fix this kind of thing for a living."

He got my meaning. First time today. "I don't like doctors."

"That's okay, don't get all knotted up over it. Look, Gary, if your car's out of gas, you go to a gas station. It doesn't matter if you like gas stations or not, you go. You go because it's where the gas is."

"I don't even have a car."

Note to self. No metaphors with Gary.

"Come on. I'm gonna have Mason give you a ride to someplace you can stay tonight. Okay?"

He lowered his head, like he'd lost the battle. "Okay."

"His car's over there. The black one."

"That's a cool car," Gary said, and he walked across the dirt road, and the lawn to the driveway and Mason's car, which we all called The Beast.

When he was out of earshot, I said, "Mason–"

"No."

"You don't get to tell me no."

"This time I do."

"He reminds me of my brother."

"He reminds *me* of *my* brother."

His brother had killed my brother, if you're keeping track.

"Mason, come on." I put my hands on his chest and looked up at him. "He's sick, not dangerous."

"Those two things are not mutually exclusive."

"Put him in the motel in town. Leave him some cash. I'll get him in with a shrink tomorrow. He needs help. This is how I want to handle it, Mason."

He looked at me hard and there were so many arguments he could've made. Like what about the boys, and my sister, and her kids, and so on. But he didn't. He blew air through clenched teeth, and said, "Fine. I'll put him in the motel. One night, Rache. We get him hooked up with social services and mental health, and leave his ass back in the city. You can put him up at the Hilton if you want, but there. Not here. Okay?"

"Okay. And thank you."

He looked like he wanted to say more, but he didn't. He went and got in the car, started it up. It had this deep, loud rumble to it that testified to my man's manliness as he drove the homeless, helpless, slightly scary Gary to a motel about a mile from our front door.

Yeah, Mason was probably right. I might've made a bad call just then. I hoped not.

"Gary Conklin, right? You have a middle name?" Mason asked.

"Robert."

"Gary Robert Conklin. Nice. And you're what, twenty-four, twenty-five?"

"I turned twenty-three my last birthday."

"And when was that?"

"July."

Close enough for a background check. "Where were you staying before the shelter, Gary?"

He broke eye contact, stared out the window.

Mason gave him several seconds, but when he didn't answer, had to move on. It was a short drive to the motel. Too short, if you asked him. "You told Rachel you don't like doctors. So you've seen doctors before, then?"

"Everybody's seen doctors before."

"Who was the last doctor you saw, Gary? Do you remember his name?"

"Her name," Gary said.

Mason thought Rachel would have kicked him for exhibiting subconscious remnants of sexism. He was woke, he swore he was.

"Dr. Guthrie. But she was wrong."

"Do you take medicine, Gary?"

"I shouldn't have gone to your house," he said.

They pulled into the motel lot, and Mason headed into the office to get the kid a room. When he came back out, Gary was standing next to the car, arms full of leftovers in Tupperware.

Mason held up the key. "Got you a room for the night," he said, walking while he talked. It was only across the parking lot. He unlocked the door to room twelve and opened it wide, stepping inside with Gary right behind him.

The fan unloaded his leftovers onto a small table, and Mason said, "There's a little fridge over there to put the food in for the night, and here's your key."

"Why do I have to stay?"

"Because Rachel wants to help you make your life better."

"She thinks I'm crazy, doesn't she? I'm not, you know. I just have bad thoughts."

"They make a pill for that."

Gary frowned hard, like he was working a jigsaw puzzle in his scrambled-up head. The poor guy. Mason sighed and tried to be kinder. "Nobody thinks you're crazy. Sometimes you get sick, you take medicine, you get better. There's nothing crazy about that, kid. That's life, is what that is. That's all. It happens to everybody from time to time."

"It does?"

"It does. I'll see you in the morning, okay Gary?"

"Okay."

We relaxed on our balcony that night, Mason and me, in our comfy robes, with drinks in hand. There was a lopsided, almost full moon rising over the reservoir, and the little bit of vodka in my Coke was smoothing out all my rough edges.

Jeremy and Misty had invited Josh and Christie to go to the newest Marvel movie with them. Christie had laughed and rolled her eyes. Josh lit up like Times Square on New Year's Eve. So we had the place to ourselves–you know, aside from the two bulldogs snoring like bull*dozers* on our bed.

"Alone at last," I said, taking a nice big sip while regretting that it was two thirds of the way gone. "I hate to bring it up while we're in such a beautiful moment–"

"Then don't."

I looked at him and smirked. "We *have* met, right?" He closed his eyes, resolved himself to the inevitable. "Tell me about the body today."

He sighed, but he talked. "White male, mid-fifties, once-red hair going gray. You know how that looks?"

"I know exactly how that looks." Having seen it up close while I strangled him. "Cause of death?"

"Don't know yet. But there were ligature marks."

"What about the car?"

"Yeah, you nailed that, too. Jaguar in the parking area at the trailhead. Car's registered to a Dwayne Clark of Dilmun, a small lake town just past Ithaca."

"Shit."

He understood the thousand-and-one emotions conveyed by the single word. He was the only one who possibly could.

"Any forensics?"

"Wrapped in burlap."

"Burlap. Burlap. Burlap..." I snapped my fingers at him. "The Craig's List Ripper!"

"Hasn't been active since the nineties."

"How can anyone say that for sure?"

"No bodies found since twenty-eleven."

"He's hiding them better."

"They were all women."

"All but one."

"Right, but that one was in drag," Mason pointed out.

"You think the burlap's coincidence, then?" I bounded out of my chair.

My drink sloshed dangerously, so I downed it and headed inside for my phone. Unlike Mason, I respected my no-devices-on-the-balcony rule. I grabbed it off the nightstand, started tapping, and found what looked like a decent report on the Craig's List Ripper.

I scrolled with my thumb, speed reading while Mason looked over my shoulder. "Look at this crime scene." I tapped on a photo where one of the serial killer's victims had been found.

"It's very similar," Mason said, spreading the image larger, really studying it. "This might be better on the desktop."

"Way ahead of you." We hurried through the house. My office was the 30' by 30' third floor in the peak of the house, with its own mini balcony. Its front was entirely glass and faced the reservoir. My desk was on the back wall, facing the front and all that glass, with a desktop and a laptop ready to roll.

I sat, and he stood behind me, looking over my shoulder as I read aloud.

"The Craig's list Ripper, also known as the Long Island Killer, the Gilbo Beach Killer, blah blah blah. Yes. They were all strangled. Several bodies found near water."

"Not all in burlap, though. Not all in one piece, either."

"There's no such thing as coincidence, Mason."

"We're five hours away from his dumping ground."

"We're five hours away from *one* of his dumping grounds. The only one we know of." I looked up at him, daring him to argue.

"What are you doing, babe?" He tucked my hair behind my ear. "Internet research? That's not your forte. What does your NFP tell you?"

I shrugged. "Nothing about *this* guy."

"I didn't think so."

I pushed away from the computer, got up from my chair and paced across the room, closing my eyes and trying to recall the dream or vision or whatever the hell it had been. "It felt like a woman. And there was...there was a needle," I said snapping my fingers, because I'd just remembered it. "She drugged him first. We need to get to that body and check for a track mark in the crease under the left butt cheek."

"I'm meeting the new forensic pathologist in the morning. Come with me."

"To an autopsy?"

"Autopsy's already done. She texted me an hour ago."

"Okay, Mason. I'll go with you. Right after we get Gary squared away."

"I left him fifty bucks," he said. "He's not gonna be there in the morning. He's gonna go spend it to get high."

"If you felt the shit storm inside his head, you'd want to self-medicate, too."

"Not judging. Just saying."

"He came here because he wanted me to help him. He's gotta stick around long enough to let me."

He hugged me close. He'd shucked his robe, and mine was open, so I got that warm, silky rub of skin against skin. I wrapped my arms around his waist and laid my cheek on his chest.

CHAPTER 3

"Happy Labor Day weekend, right?" asked the twelve-year-old pixie, standing over the open chest of a dead guy in the basement of Our Lady of Lourdes Memorial Hospital.

Mason had told me she looked like a Christmas elf, and he had nailed it.

"Rachel, meet Billie Carmichael, forensic pathologist."

She beamed at me. "It's a pleasure, Ms. de Luca. I'm excited to work with you." Her eyes slid to Mason, who stood on my left, then quickly back to me. I got, *did I do okay?*

I got it. She was a fan and he'd advised her not to gush, but it was oozing from her pores. She was doing a good job trying to hide it, though.

"Have you run toxicology?" I needed to get a look at the crease under his left butt cheek without her noticing, or she'd want to know how I knew. My NFP was a closely-guarded secret. Oh, there was gossip. I hated that there was, but there was. I'd been too close to too many gruesome murder investigations for there not to be. And you know, as far as the general public is concerned, woo-woo is woo-woo. If you're a self-help author you must also be a fortune teller, brandishing crystals and reading palms.

"Toxicology is in process," she said. "Everything else is done. Just gotta sew him up and release him to the funeral home. Widow's called three times already."

Note to self, widow's in a hurry. That probably wasn't so unusual, though.

"The cause of death was asphyxia by strangulation. Killer used twisted wire. Twice. From behind him, and from in front of him. We got a few shards of metal off the skin. You can see the pattern there in his neck." She poked the skin on the dead guy's neck with a gloved-forefinger.

I grimaced like that bothered me, and I didn't have to fake too hard. The memory of choking the life out of this human being was vivid and sickening. Here he was, dead. A life extinguished. And it felt like I'd been the one to extinguish it. "I have to step out," I said, holding one palm up. I hurried out of the room, and when Mason tried to follow, I said, "No, stay. I'll be back, I just need a breath of death-free air."

I tried to tell him I was up to something with my eyes, and he probably read it, along with my disgust and remorse for something I hadn't even done. He was way better at reading me than I was at reading him, which is ironic when you think about it.

I went out of the room into the hallway, and up one level to get a signal. Then I called the main desk. Someone answered, and I said, "Page Dr. Carmichael. It's urgent." They put me on hold.

I ran back down the stairs. By the time I was at the cutting room doors, I was distracted from my guilt trip and also aware I needed to exercise once in a while. Billie Carmichael was hurrying out the double doors to answer the fake call on the nearest in-house phone. She breezed past me, saying, "Be right back." Then she hit the stairs with effortless speed. The nearest landline was right at the top.

I rushed back into the room and over to Dwayne Clark on the table, and I slammed the door on my sickening feelings by focusing on the immediate need. "Get over here and help me roll him."

Mason grabbed a pair of gloves, struggled his big hands into them, and rolled the guy up onto his side. I grabbed a glove too, snapped it on and reached for his butt cheek. Mason looked horrified.

I lifted the guy's cheek, adjusting the overhead light with my free hand. "Look. Right there. That's where I injected him in the dream or whatever."

Elf steps pitter-pattered just outside the door.

"Put him back, put him back," I whisper-shouted.

Mason dropped the guy, yanked off his gloves, and

stuffed them into a red bin. I remembered I was still wearing one and put that hand behind my back as Billie Carmichael came into the room.

"No one on the phone," she said. "Probably the widow again. Anyway, back to the victim. There are bruises on his back." She tapped the tablet that was on a nearby stand, bringing up some photos of the corpse—a far more efficient method than rolling him over like we'd done. "You can clearly see the two round bruises on his back. Made before he died, but I'm damned if I know how."

"Looks like someone was kneeling on him," Mason said.

Her brows rose, and she looked at him like she'd just realized he was the one true Santa.

I sent him a death-glare for taking credit for my shit while still trying to peel off the glove behind my back. I was not having any luck.

"Let us know when you get the tox screen back," Mason said.

"I'll text you," she promised, looking at the body, then frowning, and looking at us again. He hadn't landed in precisely the same position, and the light wasn't pointing where it had been, either.

The glove I'd been tugging on for a full minute came off my hand suddenly, and made a loud snap.

"We have to run," Mason said. "Thanks, Billie." He grabbed me by the hand, and tugged me behind him out of the room.

At the top of the stairs, he said, "The garotte. Kneeling on his back. The injection site. You got a lot of detail in that dream, Rache." We stepped out into the late morning sunshine and fresh air.

"Too much. It's creepy."

We got into his car. He reached across the space between us, smoothed back my hair, then cradled my head in his big hand. "I wish it wasn't this hard on you. But it's gonna be okay. You know that, right?"

The tension in me dissolved just because he'd touched me and told me it was going to be okay. Did I have it bad, or what?

So when was the idiot going to pop the big question?

My God, you are gagging me.

I'm gagging myself, Inner Bitch. Can't be helped.

"I know it'll be okay," I said. "I'm good. I mean, it's what I do, right? It's my gift."

"And your curse."

"Thanks, Mr. Monk." He got the reference, which made us both smile. "Can we look around for Gary now?"

"The kids–"

"Josh was picked up shortly after we left. Today was the Hershey Park thing."

"Chuckie's birthday trip. Right."

"And Jeremy's spending his Sunday reconnecting with his high school friends. I told him it was okay. Because we have to share him whether we like it or not. Like grownups."

He made a face at me.

"The dogs will be okay for a couple more hours," I said. "Let's check the shelters for Gary."

"While I drive," he said, "Find a psychiatrist named Dr. Guthrie. Maybe she'll talk to me."

"To us," I corrected.

"To me," he said. "You don't have the equipment."

"A dick?" I asked, widening my eyes at him.

"A *badge*." All fake-shocked at my gutter brain. God, I loved him.

***

Mason sat in Dr. Melissa Guthrie's waiting room. The receptionist was behind glass. There was a fish tank and a patient in the waiting room with him. The patient was a brunette about forty with worry lines around her eyes. They'd exchanged a nod. He'd thrown in a smile. She hadn't reciprocated.

Once she'd found Guthrie's office address, Rachel had dropped him off and headed out to check the shelters. Mason didn't like it, but you couldn't really argue with her once she'd made up her mind. And she'd made up her mind.

A closed door opened, a woman leaned out and said, "You can come in Detective Brown. Gloria, I'll only be ten minutes. Okay?"

The worried brunette nodded.

Mason wished Rachel was there to tell him how pissed off she was. "It won't even take ten minutes," he told her as he got up, even though it might.

Dr. Guthrie reminded Mason of his mother. She had the same lean frame, dignified manner, and chic white-silver hair. His mom's was shorter and not as curly. Mason flashed his badge and said, "I need to talk to you about Gary Conklin."

"You can talk to me about anyone you want. I can't talk back." She tipped her head to one side. "So? Talk."

"My um...significant other is Rachel de Luca."

"Oooh." The sound she made spoke volumes. Mason had no doubt what the psychiatrist thought of self-help gurus like Rachel. "I've read her."

Non-committal as hell. "Gary is a fan," he said.

"Several of my clients are fans."

"Well, this one showed up at our home yesterday, in Whitney Point. Said he walked there from Binghamton."

"Oh, my." She lifted her silver brows. "Well, I'm concerned too, then. But Detective, let me ease your mind. I don't think Gary's dangerous. I really don't. He's a sweet young man."

"Thank you for that."

"I'm fond of him."

"We got him a room for the night, but he was gone this morning. Do you think you could check in on him?"

"If you know where he is, of course I will."

"We're working on that right now. I got the feeling he was off his meds. Can you tell me when you last saw him?"

"I'm afraid not." She took a card off her desk and handed it to him. "Let me know when you find him."

He took the card and headed out, texting Rachel on his way to the elevator. "Any luck?"

"None. You?"

"Pick me up," he tapped. "I'll fill you in."

Jeremy and Mason took the pontoon boat out on the lake for some Sunday afternoon fishing. After catching up with his friends all morning, Jere had come home and actually asked Mason to hang out with him. If I was sappier, I'd have teared up. I didn't mind being left out. They needed the one-on-one time, and besides, I wanted the house to myself. I wanted to delve into every detail I could remember about that dream, disturbing as it was. And everything since. I was missing something, I knew I was.

I took a long, steamy shower, put on my most comfy cuddly fleece, and brewed a cup of herbal tea. Chamomile. It had been a Christmas present from a new editor, and still hadn't been opened. I silenced all the ringers in the house, and put a big silk pillow on the floor of my office. *I* was going to meditate. Woo-woo is woo-woo, right? Might as well play the part.

Not long ago, a phony psychic had taught me her method for "opening the channels," as she called it. And even though I'd pegged her for a fraud, I'd given it a try, cause my shit was on the fritz, and she hadn't tried to kill me yet. That came later. To my utter shock, it had actually worked.

So, I assumed the position, or what I thought was the position. Sitting on a soft pillow with my legs crossed, guru-style. I took a few deep, calming breaths, followed by a blissful sip of my herbal tea, and then I spat it all over the place.

"Ohmy*gawd*, that stuff is awful!"

I was on my feet and back in the kitchen in three point five seconds. I rinsed the cup and poured it full of coffee from the pot, added abundant quantities of French Vanilla creamer that was neither fat-free nor sugar-free. I am nothing if not a rebel. Then I headed back to my office.

Tea had seemed to go with the whole Natalia DaVine open the channels thing, until I remembered—I *detest* tea.

So I sipped my coffee—nectar of the gods—and got all comfortable. Closing my eyes, I imagined a spiral staircase descending into the ground. I tried to remember which color the first step was supposed to be. Red, that was it. So I stepped onto the red step, and—

He was a malignant tumor that had to be excised from the world.

The words echoed up at me from the bottom of my imaginary staircase, and my eyes popped open. I said it again, out loud, so I'd remember, word for word. "He was a malignant tumor that had to be excised from the world." Aiming my gaze ceilingward, I said, "Damn, Natalia. That shit really works. I guess even a murderous bitch like you isn't an entire waste of oxygen. Or wasn't. May you rest in peace. Sorry I shot you, by the way."

Meditation, complete.

I pulled my laptop over and typed the phrase into the search bar.

It was a line from an old movie starring Reginald D'Voe, arguably the greatest horror movie actor of all time. That voice. Those eyes. He'd died just a couple weeks ago, too. Was that coincidence?

There's no such thing as coincidence.

You're right, IB, there's not.

I Googled Reginald D'Voe and found about a dozen obituaries, all of which agreed that he had lived and died in the place he loved most, his gothic mansion in the small Finger Lakes town of Dilmun, NY.

The same town the late Dwayne Clark, recently strangled in the back of his Jag while I knelt on his back, was from.

Inner bitch and I had an identical reaction. *What the actual fuck?*

I could barely wait to tell Mason my news. But Josh returned from his fun-park trip, juggling carnival prizes and a three-foot-tall alien with a straw in its head. I estimated it had a soda capacity of approximately three gallons.

Okay, one.

"You are sunburned," I said. "You didn't even take that sunblock I packed out of your backpack, did you?"

He grinned at me, white rings around his eyes. "Nope."

"I didn't think so. You have fun, though?"

"We rode the Skyrush like six times! It's awesome." Then he looked around, "Did Jeremy go back?"

"He's outside with your Uncle. They caught enough fish for supper this afternoon. They're cleaning and cooking tonight."

"I'll help!" Backpack, stuffed animals, and a four-foot alien fell like autumn leaves as he raced through the house and out the back door. The dogs raced after him, and I had to lunge to catch the door before they went out.

"Uh-uh, no way. No fishy dog breath. Not today, my friends." Myrtle sighed and plodded back to her favorite sleeping spot, a plush doggy bed I had to replace every few months because no one had the brains to make one with a waterproof inside, and a removable, washable outside. Yet. The results of their froggy hunting expeditions were constantly soaking their beds.

I worked on my newest self-help book while they

made dinner, and actually got quite a bit done. Natalia, the late murderous fraud from hell, had inspired a section about every life having value, no matter how poorly it was lived. Good stuff.

By the time Josh yelled, "It's ready, Aunt Rache!" so loud I could hear him on the third floor, I had the new section hammered out, and emailed it to Amy with a "tell me what you think of this" note.

We ate together at the actual dining room table. Everyone had enjoyed their day. I got to hear Jeremy and Mason's moment-by-moment recap of their fishing trip, and Joshua's excited retelling of his day at Hershey Park. There were thirteen roller coasters, but only three worthy of Josh and his pals' time waiting in line.

Mason and the boys and I had gone there once. It had been a crushing disappointment for me. It was hot. It was crowded—mostly with idiots. And it turned out that the park was not, in fact, made of chocolate. That name is false advertising.

The fish was so good we cleaned the platter. I convinced the kids to take the dogs for a walk, waved them off, closed the door, turned to Mason and said, "I got something!"

"So did I," he replied, and he looked like he'd been waiting as impatiently as I had.

I said, "You first," as we headed into the kitchen to stack dishes in the dishwasher. Then I looked around in surprise. "There's not oil and flour everywhere. What gives?"

"The guys and I tag teamed it. I cooked, they cleaned up as I went along."

"*That* is a *good* system!"

"Hey. I'll have you know sloppy cooks are the best cooks."

"I'm going to embroider that on an apron for you someday. Coffee?"

"Yes."

I put on a cup of decaf.

"Rosie texted me the background on the victim," Mason said.

"Dwayne Clark of Dilmun, New York."

He picked up on my excitement and paused. "Yes. Why'd you say it like that?"

"You first. Tell me the rest."

His eyebrows did that bendy thing they do when he's trying to figure out some odd thing I've said. I loved that bendy thing.

"Dwayne Clark," he said at length, "Was *recently* of Dilmun, New York. He moved to an apartment in Binghamton a few weeks ago. He and his wife Juanita were in the middle of a divorce. And there was a nasty a custody battle over their six-year-old son, Juan."

"Wait, Juanita named her kid Juan?" I asked. "Isn't that a little Norma and Norman Bates-ish?"

"Aha! Sexist!" he said, pointing at me.

"You're right. It is."

Oh, he looked so smug. "We'll meet them tomorrow. We're going to the funeral."

"Tomorrow's Labor Day, babe," I moved his coffee out of the way, stuck my mug in its place on the one-cup brewer, and deftly switched out the coffee pods. Reusable ones. They were a gift from Misty, who said if we didn't use them, we hated the planet, so you know, we caved. "It's Josh's last day before starting seventh grade."

"I haven't forgotten that for a minute," he said. "Fortunately, the service isn't until seven. We'll have the whole day with the boys. And you don't have to go if you don't–"

"The hell I don't. You need me."

"That, I do." He sipped his coffee. I was jealous that mine wasn't done yet. "What did you get today?" he asked.

"I decided to do the Natalia meditation."

"With the spiral staircase?"

"Right. I barely got my big toe on the first step when I remembered what the killer was thinking. Well, not remembered exactly. It just sort of played in my head. Like an ad in the middle of a Youtube video. Unwanted, from outside. And what it said was, 'He was a malignant tumor that had to be excised from the world.' So I Googled the phrase, just in case it was something. I mean it was so precise. It felt memorized, not organic. Not to me and not to whoever was thinking it."

"And what did Detective Google say?"

My coffee was done. I took it, added my French V—though it was darn near time for Pumpkin Spice—stirred three times and took a delicious sip. Then I said, "It's a line from an old horror movie, *The Devil's Lambs,* starring Reginald D'Voe." I sipped some more, savoring the coffee as much as the telling.

Mason frowned, clearly unsure where I was going. "Didn't he die recently?"

"Two weeks ago." I tapped my phone to bring up the page I'd saved, and turned it his way. The headline read: "Small-town Dilmun, New York plans monument to its most famous resident, the late great Reginald D'Voe."

I'd already read the story, of course. Some in Dilmun wanted to memorialize the actor with a statue depicting his role as The Headless Horseman. There was a sketch of a rearing horse with a cape-wearing body, sans head.

The head was cradled in the crook of the actor's arm, but instead of the sinister sneer and sharply crooked brow the world had come to know and love, this face wore a knowing smile, and was winking. The plan's opponents said it was undignified and too dark. Supporters said Reggie would've loved it. I guessed the jury was still out.

"He was from Dilmun," Mason said softly.

"And so was Dwayne Clark," I reminded him, though he clearly got it. "And the killer was thinking one of the actor's lines during the murder."

Mason nodded slowly. "Could be coincidence. Might just be that the killer is from the same town as the victim, and has probably seen a D'Voe flick or two. Maybe that's all it is."

"Okay, sure, it *could* be coincidental," I admitted. "Statistically, most killers live near their victims."

"Usually *with* their victims," he said.

"And people from Dilmun might be more into D'Voe horror flicks than most. But then why do I keep getting it?"

"Maybe it's just—"

"'He was a malignant tumor that had to be excised from the world.' My stuff keeps hitting the Play button on that line. And I don't get random shit. You know that, Mason. If I'm getting this, then it means something. Jeeze, where have you been the last two years?"

"Okay." He held up both hands.

Yeah, I'd been sliding into pissed off. I hadn't asked for this thing, but I had it. It was real and it was a part of me. And if Mason didn't believe in it one hundred percent, then he didn't believe in me. And that hurt.

Yes, I was over-sensitive on the issue. The merest hint of him doubting my stuff sent me into an indignant, offended, wounded spiral.

"Okay," he said again. "I didn't think that far into it. You're right. If you're getting this, it's for a reason. Maybe we'll find out more at the funeral."

I lowered my bristles and sipped my coffee. "Did Jeremy mention a problem with one Professor Asshat?"

"Professor Ashton. And yes, we talked about it this afternoon, out on the water. It was a good day."

"I know it was. I'm glad." I clinked my coffee mug to his. "So he never gave me the details. What did Professor Asshat do?"

"Gave an assignment to write about a personal trauma in the form of a police report. He told the class to pick the most emotional experience of their lives, and then write it, leaving all emotion out of it."

"That's kind of cruel."

"I think it's kind of brilliant. Cops have to learn to keep their emotions out of their work."

"Writing about a trauma reactivates it in your psyche, and therefore, in your life," I said, quoting one my own tomes, though I'd be pressed to say which one. "He's had so many traumas. Which one did he pick?"

"He wrote about his mother abducting him and Josh last year."

"Oh *hell* no."

"The professor accused him of making it up. Gave him a zero."

I got off the sofa. "Are you fucking kidding me? Hand me my phone. Who does this asshole think he is? Ashton, you said?"

"Jeremy doesn't want us to do anything," Mason said. He gave my sweater a tug and I sat back down beside him. "He says he's a man now and can handle his own shit."

"But he can't, though. We both know he can't. Do you think he's...okay?"

"I think he's shaky."

I closed my eyes. "Why the hell isn't he living at home and commuting to school? He could ride in with you if he wanted."

"Because he's trying to grow up," he said. "And I think we have to let him."

I heaved a giant sigh. "Anything else?"

"He wanted to talk about Eric."

Eric? As in your dead brother, whose sons don't know he was a serial killer? I asked with my eyes.

"I changed the subject and he let it go, but...I think it'll come up again."

I tipped my head back. Our big fat sofa was there to cradle it. "Kids are *hard.*"

"Yeah they are. That's all I got."

"I'm spent." I reached for the remote and hit the search button. "I think after the boys hit the sack, we should make some popcorn and queue up a classic old horror flick," I said, as I keyed *The Devil's Lambs* into the search bar.

Girl Blue is available now.

BROWN AND DE LUCA

The Brown and de Luca Novels
1. Sleep With the Lights On
2. Dream of Danger (ultra-short online read)
3. Wake to Darkness
4. Deadly Obsession
5. Innocent Prey

Brown and de Luca Return
1. Cry Wolf
2. Girl Blue
3. Gingerbread Man (a Brown and de Luca crossover novel)
4. The Mermaid Murder

Visit: MaggieShayne.com for more information.

STAY IN TOUCH!

Follow Maggie Shayne on BOOKBUB!
Bookbub is a curated list (meaning only the good stuff) of free and deeply discounted ebooks in a daily email and on their website. No charge to readers and no upsells.

Sign up here: Bookbub.com
Follow Maggie Shayne on Bookbub here:
Maggie-Shayne on Bookbub
Never miss a freebie or discount again!

Sign up for Maggie's NEWSLETTER!
Early looks at covers, new and upcoming releases, behind the scenes trivia, dog pictures, and sometimes a recipe!

MaggieShayne.com
Sign up at the top of the page.

Join Maggie on SOCIAL!

Maggie on Facebook
Maggie Shayne Readers Group on Facebook
Maggie on Instagram
Maggie on Threads

ABOUT THE AUTHOR

New York Times bestselling author Maggie Shayne has published more than 60 novels and 23 novellas. She has written for 7 publishers and 2 soap operas, and is a 15-time RITA® Award nominee and a RITA® winner.

Maggie lives in a beautiful, century-old, happily haunted farmhouse named "Serenity" in the wildest wilds of Cortland County, NY, with her husband and soul mate, Lance. Maggie is a Wiccan high priestess, legal clergy, and an avid follower and coach of the Law of Attraction

www.ingramcontent.com/pod-product-compliance
Lightning Source LLC
Chambersburg PA
CBHW021959130726
47903CB00014B/2492